NORTH BY NORTHEAST

Haley Parsons, a school teacher on her first real vacation in years, boards the beautiful and luxurious American Orient Express for a week-long train excursion from New Orleans to Washington, D.C. But then her jewelry begins to disappear and she finds herself an unwitting player in a kidnapping and robbery attempt. The culprit is evidently aboard the train; and Jonathan Shafer, Haley's handsome, newfound love interest, is somehow involved. Who is he, really? And what part will he play in all this?

Books by Phyllis Humphrey
in the Linford Romance Library:

FALSE PRETENCES
TROPICAL NIGHTS
FREE FALL

PHYLLIS HUMPHREY

NORTH BY NORTHEAST

Complete and Unabridged

LINFORD
Leicester

First published in Great Britain?? in 2007 by
Criterion House
Palm Desert
California

First Linford Edition
published 2014

A catalogue record for this book is available
from the British Library.

ISBN 978–1–4448–1900–7

Published by
F. A. Thorpe (Publishing)
Anstey, Leicestershire

Set by Words & Graphics Ltd.
Anstey, Leicestershire
Printed and bound in Great Britain by
T. J. International Ltd., Padstow, Cornwall

This book is printed on acid-free paper

Acknowledgments

My thanks to the charming people I met on the train, and especially those who encouraged me to write this book: Andrea Rolfingsmeier, Marice Doll and Gaynor Trammer.

Also to my writer friends, ever supportive and helpful: Shirley Allen, Amy Bird, Sandy Carpenter, Barry Friedman, Barbara Gifford, Judith Hand, Pete Johnson, Marian Jones, and to the late Peggy Kirkland, who is missed.

1

Haley Parsons stared into the beauty salon's oversized mirror. A stranger stared back at her.

The eyes, nose and mouth looked like hers, but the hair made all the difference. Blonde bangs over her forehead just cleared her eyebrows; long, shiny blonde hair curled under just above her shoulders. She resembled a movie star from the forties or fifties.

'I can't do it.' She pulled off the wig and threw it onto the cluttered counter in front of her.

'Right.' Roberta, her fellow school teacher, stood at her side. 'Go like this.'

'This' was huge spots of scalp between tufts of normally brown curly hair and had become unacceptable the moment Haley had heard the hairdresser's fateful words, 'I'll have to cut the gum out, and I'm afraid — '

She was afraid?

'I can trim the rest to match so it won't be so noticeable,' the stylist offered. 'How on earth did you get bubble gum in your hair anyway?'

'Just lucky, I guess.' Haley squeezed her eyes shut to blot out the woman butchering what was left of her hair.

Roberta filled her in. 'Ever hear the expression, 'No good deed goes unpunished'? Well, our good Samaritan here agreed to watch another teacher's kindergarten class during recess. She normally teaches seventh grade,' she added, 'but no other teacher was available this afternoon.'

'So . . . ?' the stylist prompted.

'So, as far as we could figure out later, five-year-old Timmy Blake started the fiasco. He wasn't supposed to have any bubble gum in the first place, but somehow he had an entire bag of the stuff in his pocket. Pretty soon every kid wanted some and all were blowing — or trying to blow — enormous bubbles like Timmy's.'

Haley spoke without opening her

eyes. 'Before I could put a stop to it, a little girl fell off the jungle gym and scraped her knee.'

'A one-inch bandage would have been enough,' Roberta said, taking up the story again, 'but the four-year-old started howling like she was about to lose half her leg. Her screams carried all the way to the next street and she insisted she had to go to the hospital in an ambulance with sirens.'

The stylist, who had children of her own, nodded.

'By then,' Haley said, 'the bubble-gum blowing was out of control. Not just making bubbles. Some children were throwing wads of fresh-chewed bubble gum at other children, and when I tried to stop it, I got some right in the face.'

'I can see where you got it,' the stylist said, 'three wads of the sticky stuff were imbedded in your hair.'

Haley opened her eyes. The trimming the stylist had done to even it out had left her with hair less than half-an-inch long all over her head.

The tears she'd been holding in turned into a wail. 'I look like a refugee from a concentration camp. I've only a week before my vacation. What am I going to do? I can't go looking like this.'

'Well, you could always cancel your trip.' Roberta was not only a teacher in the same private school, she was also Haley's housemate, her best friend and, sometimes, surrogate mother. But she didn't sound a bit sympathetic at the moment.

'I've been planning this for a year and already paid my money. You know how much it cost.'

'How about the insurance you bought?'

'That was in case I suddenly got sick. I don't think 'a bad hair day' will work.'

'Postpone it?'

'This is my Spring break. They only schedule the tour through the Antebellum South in the Spring. And besides, my history class is just about to study the Civil War. It was perfect timing.'

'And the three little angels had perfect aiming.'

Haley wiped her eyes and frowned at

Roberta through the mirror. 'This is no time to be funny.'

Roberta picked up the wig and held it out to Haley. 'I'm not trying to be funny. Only realistic. Do you want to go on vacation looking like a prison inmate or a beautiful woman? Your choice.'

Haley stared at herself for another long moment, then reluctantly adjusted the wig on her head again.

'See, what did I tell you?' Roberta said. 'It's perfect. You're going on a glamorous train on your spring break and a blonde wig will give you a totally new look for the trip.'

'Different, for sure. But it's not me.'

'You don't have to look like a mousy school-teacher who never wears make-up and seldom sees the inside of a beauty parlor. For the first time in years you're taking a vacation — on a fancy train at that — and this wig says 'glamorous.''

'What it says is deception. I can't pretend to be something I'm not.'

'So it's deceptive, so what? Can't you be somebody glamorous at least for a week?' She took a breath and launched her scenario again. 'Trust me, this will work. Next stop, the cosmetics counter. The clerk will do a great job with your make-up. Take notes on how to do something similar yourself.'

'I don't want to learn how to apply make-up,' Haley protested, but Roberta was in her steam-roller persona, when protests were often futile.

Roberta crossed her arms over her ample bosom. 'You don't have to go overboard, but I'm older and wiser and I say you need mascara to bring out your eyes, and some color to your face. Especially with the blonde wig.'

Haley didn't protest again, just sat looking in the mirror without really seeing herself. Roberta was often right. She was older — near retirement age — and wiser, widowed and childless, and had taken speedily to the role of mother hen to Haley. Haley's own mother had been the family bread-winner, leaving Haley's upbringing mostly to her grandmother. Gran had done her duty but decried make-up as 'vanity,' 'unsuitable,' and 'unnecessary.'

Roberta turned to the hair stylist. 'We'll take the wig.'

* * *

Later, they deposited their purchases on the dressing table in Haley's room at the house they shared, and Roberta insisted she try on the wig again. She grinned broadly. 'You need to meet a man and this serves the purpose even better than I first thought.'

'No one is out there who is going to be struck giddy by me, wig and paint, or no. Secondly, I'm perfectly happy the way I am.'

'You think there aren't any Prince Charmings because you never go anywhere. When you're not at school, you're working at the shelter for abused women. No wonder you've stopped looking. You've been brainwashed to think all men are jerks and beat their wives.'

'I don't. I'm sure there are some good men in the world, but they're already taken.' Haley didn't really believe that, but her upbringing — always trying to please Gran — had made her shy. Now, at thirty-five, she recognized the trap of indoctrination she'd fallen into.

Roberta often tried to cure her of Gran's convictions and continued pleading. 'I just hope there are a few eligible men on that train. I still think you should have taken a cruise.'

'I hate modern cruise ships. They're ugly. They always called them 'floating hotels' but now they look like them — huge rectangular boxes with a million windows. Where are the decks? Where are the smokestacks?'

'They don't need smokestacks anymore, remember?' Roberta perched on the side of the bed. 'I suppose you'd prefer the Titanic, minus the iceberg of course.'

'Of course.' Haley pulled off the wig and ran her hand over what was left of her formerly short, curly hair that was somewhere between the color of cinnamon and charcoal.

'Your train trip isn't exactly cheap,' Roberta said. 'I know you haven't spent money on yourself in years, but you only go from New Orleans to Washington, and have to fly back and forth from Denver besides. You could take two cruises for what you're paying for all that.'

'But you forget I can get seasick in a rowboat and I'm claustrophobic besides.'

'You can't be claustrophobic on a huge cruise ship.'

'But, once they start moving, you can't get off. They're prisons with a chance of drowning.'

Roberta fell back on the bedspread, laughing.

'Besides,' Haley went on, 'this train trip through the South is perfect. I love the area's history. Every mile is so full of it.'

Roberta scoffed. 'Actually, you love old movies and think the world was a better place fifty years ago. That's your grandmother's influence. You need to get over it.'

Haley defended her choice of the train excursion. 'The tour will give me personal insights into what I'm going to be teaching when I get back.'

'You think a bunch of thirteen-year-olds will care?' Roberta sat upright. 'I don't know why you can't see history first-hand and meet men too.'

She hustled out of Haley's room and returned with a blue velvet box. 'Furthermore, I'm lending you my mother's antique necklace.'

Haley gasped. 'It's too valuable.'

'Look at it this way. You'll be doing it a favor. It hasn't seen the light of day for twenty years.'

Haley shook her head. 'First you chose the wig, then the make-up and now this. I expect next you'll want to pick out my wardrobe.'

'I was coming to that. You'll be on a luxury private train and you need to fit in with the other passengers, so tomorrow we go shopping for suitable clothes.'

Although Haley suspected Roberta was serious, she laughed.

From Haley's desk, Roberta picked up the wrinkled copy of *Time Magazine* that fell open automatically to the page Haley had dog-eared months before. 'It says right here in this article about the American Orient Express, quote, 'all that's missing is Cary Grant.' I know you love your DVD of that movie, *North by Northwest*, where he met Eva Marie Saint on the train and they fell in love.'

'It's a free country, isn't it? I'm allowed a guilty pleasure.'

'Well, she was blonde and wore glamorous clothes, so the next stop is the right wardrobe.'

Haley held up her hands in a gesture of mock surrender. 'I understand your plot. You're making my trip fit with all the Alfred Hitchcock movies that had blonde heroines.'

'Hitchcock didn't make all the train movies. *Silver Streak* had a blonde heroine, so did *From Russia with Love*.

I tell you, blonde is where it's at.'

She leaned in, 'You've been watching old movies all your life. Just because your grandmother loved them doesn't mean you can't watch some newer films.'

'You know I do sometimes, but Cary Grant is my absolute favorite actor and I have all of his films on DVD. *North by Northwest* is one of the best.' She thought a moment. 'But I've also seen today's Hollywood stars. Hugh Grant is sort of like Cary. So are Pierce Brosnan and George Clooney.'

'Well, you won't meet anyone like Pierce Brosnan or George Clooney if you don't dress the part now that you have the chance.'

Haley put the wig back on and strutted around the room. 'I hate to admit it, but maybe you're right.' She stopped at the mirror and smiled at her reflection. 'Hello Gorgeous.'

'By George, I think she's got it.'

Haley flopped back on the bed, laughing. 'I'll do it. I'll go on this trip and meet someone. But remember, all those movies with blonde heroines had murders in them. I might end up a blonde corpse.'

2

The taxi stopped in front of the New Orleans French Quarter hotel whose façade clearly indicated no expense had been spared to enhance its old-world atmosphere. Haley paid the driver, smoothed her skirt over her thighs and stepped out. She'd felt uncomfortably warm on the drive from the airport, having kept on the matching jacket of the suit bought especially for the trip. She had left Denver bone-chilling cold, with a thin film of snow blanketing the runways and had no problem leaving that weather behind. But she hadn't counted on New Orleans being so warm and humid in mid-March.

Perhaps the wig was partially to blame. Still unaccustomed to it, she found it became heavier and warmer as the day progressed. However, she felt certain it was the wig that caused the doorman to rush to open the hotel door for her, the bellman to reach hurriedly for her suitcase and matching tote-bag and for every other man she'd seen all day to give her admiring glances. That was a totally new experience she could learn to like. Except, of course, that she knew she was a fraud.

Nevertheless, as she crossed the flower-patterned carpeting to the front desk, and saw a long mirror on the side wall in the lobby, she couldn't resist checking her reflection. The fake hair looked as if it had grown there, even though she hardly recognized herself under the long, shiny fall of gold.

While serving to conceal what was left of her own hair, Haley hadn't fully realized the wig's effect. She was too practical to think she'd turn into a swan or that anyone even remotely like a Cary Grant look-alike would gravitate to her on the train just because she had become an ersatz blonde. As she had assured Roberta, her goal was to enjoy the change of scenery in a different part

15

of the country and learn something she could pass on to her students.

To Roberta, on the other hand, the very idea of train travel — and on something called the 'Orient Express' — conjured up visions of Agatha Christie intrigue, and she insisted Haley should welcome all adventurous aspects.

'I dare you to pretend to be a glamorous blonde for seven days,' Roberta had said the day they bought the wig.

'Don't be silly.'

'I mean it.' Roberta added the clincher. 'If you do it — if you really wear the wig all the time with no cheating — you get to keep my mother's necklace.'

'I couldn't. It's an heirloom — ' Haley began.

'You know I had no children, no one to pass it on to. We've been friends for so long, I want you to have it. But only if you keep your side of the bargain.'

'And if I don't?'

'Then when you come home, you have to go to every singles dance I tell you about for the next year.'

Haley had groaned aloud. 'Okay, okay, I agree. But with any luck, I'll get murdered on the train first.'

Roberta had laughed and tossed a pillow at her.

At the front desk of the New Orleans hotel, Haley gave her name to the clerk and, after signing the registration form and receiving her room key, crossed to the concierge station. A white-haired, bespectacled man left his chair and approached her, smiling broadly.

'Can you tell me how far it is to Antoine's?' she asked.

'You wish to have dinner at Antoine's?'

'Yes, if it's possible.'

'Possible, yes. Probable, no.' He paused, a thin frown on his forehead. 'Not on a Friday night, with no reservations. Perhaps Monday.'

'Oh, dear. I'm taking the American Orient Express tomorrow, so it's tonight or never.'

'Ah, you're with the private train group.' The smile returned. 'In that case, let me make a suggestion. Other members of

17

the tour are booked here and I believe some of them also plan to dine at Antoine's tonight. Perhaps you could join them.'

She had never liked eating alone and had no need to stop and consider. Much as she wanted the experience of a meal at the world-renowned restaurant, she had dreaded the thought of facing a formally attired *maître d'* sneering at her request: 'Table for one.'

'I'd be happy to join the others, if they don't mind,'

The concierge nodded. 'I'll make the arrangements at once. Meet them here at seven o'clock. Antoine's is only two blocks away, a very short walk.'

What good luck. She'd get in without a reservation, and, at the same time, have the opportunity to meet some of her fellow passengers.

The bellman had been waiting for her in the lobby, holding her bags, and she tried to look as if she did this sort of thing all the time. Glamorous blondes always made others wait, didn't they?

Having never been a glamorous blonde before, how was she to know?

They entered an elevator and shot up to her floor. Once inside her room, she gave the bellhop a generous tip, and, after he was safely gone, pulled off the wig, slipped out of the traveling suit and lay across the bed, reviewing her new identity. Her adventure had begun, but how would it end?

★   ★   ★

Always priding herself on punctuality, Haley stepped out of the hotel elevator at exactly seven o'clock and crossed the lobby. She wore the coolest dress of the ones Roberta had selected for her, a sleeveless navy-blue chiffon over silk with a border print of lavender flowers, and — in case Antoine's kept its air conditioning at 'frigid' — a long-sleeved chiffon jacket edged in the print. It felt strange to have a skirt swirl around her legs after spending almost every day of her life in pants and flat shoes.

19

The concierge desk was deserted. No group ready to dine at Antoine's. A disappointed flutter began in her midriff. That sort of thing might happen to *her*, the real her, but surely it couldn't happen to the counterfeit blonde she had temporarily become. Her uneasiness increased, but a concierge — not the one she'd met earlier — rushed up, and a man in a midnight blue suit, white shirt and plum-colored silk tie followed. Both smiled at her.

Was Roberta clairvoyant, or was this a dream she'd wake from any minute? The man — not the concierge — was gorgeous.

He was no Cary Grant, with a cleft in his chin, but he would do until the reincarnation arrived. Handsome, easily six feet tall, lean, with dark wavy hair, he had wide-set blue eyes and a perfect nose. In her opinion, his mouth was his best feature, straight and wide, curving up a bit as if ready to laugh. Lips not too full. Men with puffy lips didn't appeal to her.

The concierge introduced him as Jonathan Shafer.

He took her hand. 'I'm happy to meet you.' His voice was low, well modulated and television-announcer warm. His handshake was firm, not too hard, not too soft.

She smiled and said, 'Are you the crowd the concierge promised?'

For once, she hadn't stuttered or embarrassed herself when introduced to a good-looking man. Instead, she had managed to get out a light, humorous connection without tripping over the words. But her heart was banging away inside her chest like a metronome gone berserk. She hadn't been in New Orleans for a day — hadn't even *begun* the train trip that Roberta insisted would most likely introduce her to Mr. Dreamboat — and, so far as she was concerned, there he stood.

She told herself to slow down, that this didn't mean a thing. The others supposed to be there for their dinner

21

excursion would arrive any moment. Probably Mr. Shafer's wife or girlfriend would appear. As she had told Roberta many times, the best ones were always taken. Besides, what good would it do to meet Mr. Right at a time when she wasn't herself, but an imposter? She should never have agreed to this charade. Didn't some poet warn against weaving a web of deceit?

3

The concierge answered Haley's earlier question. 'I'm afraid the other lady and gentleman have canceled. It seems there will be only the two of you this evening. I hope you don't mind.'

'On the contrary,' Jonathan Shafer said. 'Miss Parsons?'

'Of course not.' Would she mind dining alone with Mr. Wonderful? Would she mind winning a national lottery?

She couldn't remember having such a great meet since leaving college. She'd had fun in college, but then the supply of eligible men seemed to disappear. After graduation, she had spent more and more Saturday nights watching television and eating microwave meals. She had also reverted to her grandmother's long-ago warnings about going out at night, alone, or with strangers. Her resolve began to slip.

But the concierge had formally introduced Mr. Shafer. The man would be a passenger on the train as well, so she'd see him from time to time on the tour. Finally, according to Roberta's instructions, she needed to become adventurous and braver. However, to Haley, the crucial importance of the meet meant that, without Mr. Shafer and his reservations, she couldn't have dinner at Antoine's.

His hand protectively under her elbow, they crossed the lobby and went through the glass doors to the street. He dropped his hand when they left the hotel, and, although Haley had liked the feel of it, she supposed it wasn't necessary and he seemed the type to respect the independence of a woman traveling on her own. They walked side by side down the narrow sidewalk, past shops closed for the night with metal grates, many of them antique or furniture stores with elegant dining tables or glittering silver tea sets catching street lighting in the dimly-lit windows.

'So, you're on the Antebellum South Tour also?' her companion asked, choosing their shared destination, she decided, as a means of starting a conversation.

'I've never traveled in the Southeast before.' She hoped it sounded as if she'd been everywhere else, which, of course, she hadn't. She'd only been as far away from Denver as Chicago and New York, once each.

'I believe we go to Jacksonville first and then north to Washington. North by northeast, as it were.'

She wondered if he realized the similarity to the title of that old Cary Grant film and persuaded herself, from the twinkle in his eye and his grin, that he did.

They covered the two short blocks quickly. Haley's spirits soared at the sight of the large brick building on the opposite corner, with its wrought-iron balcony across the second floor. They crossed the street, Mr. Shafer opened one of the two narrow black doors and they entered a spacious dining room filled with white-cloth-covered tables. A round table, just inside the doors, held an enormous floral arrangement and a silver tray with souvenir menus.

'Reservation for Shafer,' he told the tuxedoed *maître d'* who approached them. 'Non-smoking, please.'

They followed the *maitre d'* through the room and down a corridor, to enter another large dining room, all pale paneled walls with mirrors and silver sconces. A monstrous crystal chandelier hung from the center of the ceiling.

A waiter materialized, seated them opposite each other at a side table and lifted Haley's napkin from where it had been creatively tucked into a water glass. He laid it across her lap, handed them each menus and disappeared.

'I hope you didn't mind my choosing a non-smoking room,' Jonathan Shafer said. 'Even if you want to smoke later, I think you'll be more comfortable here.'

'Much more. I don't smoke.'

'Neither do I.'

She pretended interest in her menu, hoping to hide the pleased smile that insisted on creeping up her face. Better and better, although she met fewer and fewer people who smoked these days. She remembered double-checking the brochure before signing up for the train trip and reading that smoking was restricted to the vestibules between cars.

'I recommend the Pompano Amandine,' he said next. 'It's a gulf fish and a house specialty.'

'Then you've been here before, Mr. Shafer.'

'Please, call me Jonathan, or, better yet, Jon. And yes, I have been here before. Years ago.'

'The pompano sounds perfect and please call me Haley.'

The waiter reappeared and Jon ordered for both of them.

'Did you live here or were you visiting?' she asked.

'Visiting, like now. I live in Portland, Oregon.' His smile made Haley's heartbeat speed up.

She remembered, in *To Catch a Thief*, Cary Grant's character came from Oregon. Or, rather, he told blonde Grace Kelly he did. Would Jonathan Shafer turn out to be like 'John Robie,' in the film, a former cat burglar? She grimaced inwardly. Roberta would probably like that idea, especially since the film had a romantic ending.

'Where do you hail from?' he asked.

'Denver.' She actually lived in a small town sixty miles away, but he would never have heard of it, so she didn't bother to be specific.

'What do you do in Denver?'

She didn't answer because, with relief, she saw the waiter returning with their salads. She needed time to frame her answer. She should tell him she taught school for a living, but how would that fit with the new fake blonde hair and fancy clothes?

He ordered wine to accompany the dinner and, when they were alone again, he returned to the question about her career. 'Let me guess — you're a model.'

A model? She smiled, as if he'd hit the proverbial nail on the head. 'Part time.' She *had* done some modeling while in college and worked during summer breaks at a women's dress shop, so she considered it somewhat true.

'Not many women travel alone,' he said, 'but I suppose models do a lot of that.'

'Some do, but my work keeps me closer to home.'

'But you're traveling alone this trip, aren't you?'

She realized he was fishing. He wanted to know if she was married or otherwise spoken for. Her breathing escalated. 'I'm not married, if that's what you mean.' She took a sip of water. 'Are you traveling alone too?'

'Yes, and I *was* married. As a matter of fact, we had dinner here on our honeymoon. But we're divorced.'

'Oh. I'm sorry.' Should she have said that? What did protocol dictate when he now sat in the same restaurant with another woman? He didn't comment right away, and she began to wonder what had happened to his marriage. Did he beat his wife until she finally left him? No, she must stop thinking along those lines. In spite of her volunteer work at the abused women's shelter, she knew that most men did not beat their wives. And this man certainly didn't appear the type who did.

He smiled over at her. 'I ordered the Pompano Amandine that time too. I thought it was delicious. My wife hated it. Said it was too bland. She disliked French food in general. Not spicy enough for her.'

Haley had always loved the delicate flavors of French cooking, couldn't imagine anyone not liking it. See, he didn't beat his wife. They were just incompatible.

He leaned across the table and looked into her eyes. 'I got over my marriage long ago. I'm sorry I brought up the subject.'

Haley tried to seem less flustered than she felt, and nibbled on her salad. 'And what do you do for a living?'

He didn't answer because the waiter returned and poured wine for him to taste before filling both glasses.

They ate for a few minutes without speaking until Jon remarked on the New Orleans weather. 'I believe it gets quite hot here in the summer, but it's very comfortable now. What's it like in Denver this time of year?'

'Cold and snowy. Do you get snow in Portland — Jon?'

'Once in a while. We can ski on Mount Hood, of course, but down in the city we get more rain than snow. That's what keeps the state green.'

Their entrées arrived and Haley tried to think of something more interesting to talk about than the weather, but what? She'd let him think she was a model, but she actually knew nothing about professional modeling. Luckily, it wouldn't be interesting to a man, anyway. Besides, she wanted to learn more about *him*, and he hadn't answered her question. Before she got up the courage to ask again, the waiter removed their dinner plates.

'Would you like to try the *Crêpes Suzette?*' Jon asked.

She hesitated.

'Please do,' he urged. 'I didn't have them the last time and I don't want to miss out again.'

Haley remembered their earlier conversation and what little she knew about *Crepes Suzette*. 'Surely your wife didn't think that was too bland?'

'Perhaps not, but she didn't want the attention.' He turned to the waiter and said they'd have the crepes and coffee.

'Attention?' Haley asked. 'I don't understand.'

'You will in a moment.'

She only smiled and, when the waiter poured her coffee, she sipped some. Suddenly remembering he hadn't answered her question, she started to ask it again when the lights in the room dimmed to a soft glow and the waiter maneuvered a cart to their table.

On the cart stood a chafing dish containing four rolled up crepes in a sauce garnished with orange slices. The waiter poured what Haley supposed was brandy over the crepes and flicked an automatic lighter.

Blue flames erupted from the dish, and the waiter lifted and tilted the pan, spooning the flaming sauce over the crepes time after time. Next, he spooned what appeared to be the fire itself, into the air and onto the table-cloth, a cascade of blue flames. She stared, transfixed.

In moments, the show ended, the waiter turned to the patrons in the rest of the dining room, bowed and said, 'Did you enjoy the performance?' They applauded.

Someone returned the room lights to their former level of brightness and the waiter deftly arranged crepes onto their plates.

Haley grinned at Jon. 'I see what you mean about 'attention.''

Coffee and crepes finished, Jon said he'd pay the dinner bill. 'My treat.'

'Oh, I couldn't let you do that. I'm grateful you had a reservation so I could come here at all.'

'And I'm delighted you could come. Just think how awful it would have been if I'd had to dine alone.' He grinned. 'People would talk.'

'But — '

'Please allow me.' He put his hand over hers where she had reached across the table. 'Besides, there's always the old expense account.'

'Well — if you insist.' She relaxed. If his business required the trip on the train and he could write off his meals, it would be all right. She hoped his company tolerated hundred-dollar dinners.

When they left the restaurant, he had her turn right instead of left and walked her to Bourbon Street, which had been blocked off to automobile traffic and sported crowds of people.

'Do they do this every night?' she asked.

'I don't know, but it's fine by me.'

This time, he tucked her arm into the bend of his. It felt comfortable and they strolled down the center of the street, glancing from side to side at the various shops and cafes, most of which still remained open for business.

Haley had always heard Bourbon Street was the home of New Orleans jazz, but in the one block they walked, saw only two small nightclubs, their doors standing open to the balmy weather and the milling crowds, playing jazz. All the rest seemed to be playing hard rock, noisy and without discernible melody. Nor were all the businesses nightclubs or cafes. The street also held dozens of souvenir shops selling everything from post cards to tee shirts.

'New Orleans is just what I expected,' she said. 'I find it hard to believe a hurricane devastated the city not so long ago.'

'We're in the French Quarter, which, fortunately was spared the worst of Katrina. Many other areas weren't quite so lucky.'

Haley returned to her earlier question. 'Just what is it you do? What corporation am I indebted to for dinner tonight?'

'Don't worry. They can afford it.' He changed the subject. 'Would you like an after-dinner drink?'

She glanced around but saw no place in which she wanted to spend any time. Way too noisy. Through the open doors, she could see people jammed together, and the decibel level seemed high enough to kill birds. 'Not now, thanks.'

At the next corner, Jon steered her left and, one short block later, they were back in front of the hotel. As they climbed the three shallow steps to the lobby, Haley hoped he'd suggest going into the hotel lounge and having a drink there, but he apparently wanted to call it a night or thought she did. She couldn't think of what to say, and he escorted her straight to the elevator.

When they reached her room, he unlocked the door with her key and gave her hand a gentle squeeze. 'I'm glad you accompanied me tonight. I had no idea I'd be meeting someone so charming and such a delightful dinner companion. I had a great time.'

'I enjoyed it too. Thank you.' She groaned at sounding like a country hick again. But what did blondes say at times like this that brunettes didn't? Probably they would invite him in. Probably a real blonde would have rented a suite, not just a standard bedroom.

'It's nice to know I'll see you tomorrow,' he said.

Yes. She'd be seeing him the next day, and she felt certain he liked her. Roberta had been right to insist she buy the new clothes, and, especially, the wig. Blondes really did have more fun.

He walked back toward the elevator and she closed the door, then leaned against the inside, remembering the admiring way he had looked at her all evening.

Shortly, her strong hold on reality kicked in. Sure, she had hoped to have a great time on this trip, and maybe — just maybe — live up to Roberta's expectations that she'd meet someone. But, how could it have happened so quickly? Real life never worked like that evening. Not *her* life anyway. It was just too good to be true.

In fact, it hadn't been true. She wasn't a beautiful blonde model, but a plain, brown-haired schoolteacher. Furthermore, he might not be who he seemed either. He had never answered her questions about him. What did *he* have to hide? It would be just her luck that, when she'd finally met a handsome bachelor, he'd turn out to be — her imagination headed straight to the last movie she'd seen — a Mafia hit man.

4

At three o'clock the next afternoon, Haley's taxi dropped her off at the train station and she carried her bags to the long table behind which stood three young women in navy-blue blazers. One checked her name off a list, the second fastened a tag to her suitcase and put it with a group of others, and the third selected one from the row of blue badges laid out on the table.

'Please wear this when you board the train at four o'clock,' the woman said, 'and all the time you're on the train and on our various excursions.'

Haley examined the identification badge for a moment, noticing her name engraved in white on it, along with the logo of the private luxury train: the letters AOE inside a lavishly decorated oval, with scrollwork below and lions rampant. She pinned it to the lapel of her jacket, then turned and found a seat in the terminal to wait.

She shook her raincoat before placing it across the empty seat next to her, glad she'd brought it when she had to dodge raindrops on the way back to the hotel that afternoon. When she'd returned from her day of sightseeing, the rain came down in earnest and, even now, the gray sky sent rain slanting past the large windows that lined the side of the terminal building.

She surveyed the other passengers beginning to gather. Roberta's insistence that she'd meet a man on the trip surfaced, and, although she hated to admit it, Haley hoped to see Jonathan Shafer. After his seeming interest the night before, she half expected an early phone call inviting her to breakfast or lunch or sightseeing — at the very least a shared taxi ride to the station — but that hadn't happened. Instead, she walked to a café for New Orleans' specialties: *beignets* and *café au lait*. Then she'd taken a bus tour of the city, where some trees still sported strings of beads left over from *Mardi Gras.* Too bad she'd had no one to share it with.

After a few more glances around without spotting Jon, Haley got up and went into the ladies' room, checking once more on her appearance in the blonde wig. A memory from her school days returned, a time when she complained to her mother that she wasn't pretty and boys didn't come up and ask her to dance at the Friday parties.

Mother had said, 'You are pretty, but even if you weren't, it wouldn't be important. Having a good personality is much better.'

'But,' she had wailed, 'how will they ever know I have a good personality if they never come near me?'

'Beauty,' Mother had said, 'is only what gets a boy from over there to over here. Once they're over here, you'd better have more than that to keep them around.'

Of course she was right, and Haley

finally had boyfriends of her own. But none of them had been Mr. Right and now she was thirty-five years old and still unmarried. She wished it didn't matter — she'd often said that to Roberta — but it did. Her biological clock ticked loudly and, much as she loved teaching other people's children, she wanted a baby of her own while still possible. And she wouldn't have one without a husband as well. She always thought it selfish to deliberately have a child who would never know its real father. So, on the whole, she supposed she might as well resign herself to the fact that it might never happen.

But now she had let Roberta talk her into buying the wig and the fancy clothes and learned the latest make-up techniques, all to get a man from over there to over here. And what good had it done? After the dinner with Jon, he'd evaded her questions and promptly disappeared. Perhaps he wasn't even a passenger on the Orient Express. Face it, this make-believe blonde had not met someone after all.

She sighed, left the restroom and returned to the waiting area in time to see the huge metal gates which separated the waiting area from the trains slide open. Six tall young men in navy-blue uniforms with gold braid, wearing white gloves, came through the gates and lined up in front of them. A feminine voice on the public address system announced that each passenger would be called by name and escorted to his or her train carriage and compartment. So this was really going to be as charmingly old-fashioned as she'd hoped. She'd stepped into the past.

Most of the people waiting in the terminal stood up and names were called. Haley gathered her belongings, slinging the strap of her black leather handbag over her shoulder, and picking up her coat and tote-bag. After about twelve other people responded and joined their escorts to be taken to the train, Haley heard her name called and did the same. So did another woman and a fiftyish-looking couple.

'My name is Alan — ' the young man announced. As they strolled alongside the train, Haley barely heard him, her attention fastened on the train itself. First the last car, with its rounded, multi-windowed rear coach, and then a long string of shiny cars, each a light cream color on the upper half, and royal blue below with that same logo in gold on the side, ' — and I'll be your porter in the Istanbul sleeping car.'

Istanbul! What luck, she'd been assigned to a car with the same name as the city the original Orient Express visited. The adventure just got better and better.

They hadn't walked far when Alan stopped at an entrance where another uniformed man waited to help them onto a portable step and then up into the car. 'Follow me,' Alan said, and turned left after mounting. The married couple — Haley seemed to remember their names were Jackson — climbed aboard first, and then the other woman, Mrs. Draper — short, plump, and seemingly in her sixties — who, like her, traveled alone. Haley brought up the rear of their little group.

As she traveled the narrow carpeted corridor with its closed doors on the left and large windows on the right, she heard snatches of Alan's instructions. He said something about the letters above the doors indicating their compartment, and after the passengers in front of her disappeared into narrow doors, Alan directed her to 'E' cabin, and she turned into a small room seemingly in the very center of the carriage.

The size didn't shock her. Thanks to the pictures in the colorful brochure the company had sent, she expected it to be small, and saw her suitcase already inside, resting on the long comfortable-looking couch covered in a blue-gray fabric. Of course, she could have signed up for a larger compartment, but — even if she'd been willing to spend more money to impress anyone — they'd already been booked by couples.

And this had plenty of room for one person. The couch would turn into her bed at night, a large window took up most of the available space on the wall opposite the door, and, across from the couch, inset into the expanse of gleaming dark walnut, stood a stainless steel sink with a three-panel mirror above. A narrow door next to that held a hook on the back of which hung a fluffy white terry-cloth robe with the train logo embroidered in blue and gold on the upper left side. Opening the door, she found a toilet room with about the same maneuvering space as the ones on airplanes.

Alan, apparently finished helping the other three passengers, knocked on the open door and stuck his head inside, a wide grin on his youthful face.

He pointed to the two bottles in holders next to the sink. 'Bottled water,' he said. 'Although the tap water is perfectly safe to drink.'

'Telephone,' he said next, and Haley

saw a black handset on the wall. 'It's not for outgoing calls,' he added. 'It just goes to the office, which is in the Seattle club car, two carriages that way.' He pointed. 'Someone is there twenty-four hours a day, and you can use it to make reservations for the shower room at the end of the car. That way you'll be sure it's clean and ready for you.'

'I see,' Haley said.

'Closet.' He pointed to the opening in the wall next to the door. 'Drawers for your clothes.' He came inside and stooped down to show her two plastic drawers that pulled out from under the couch, and a third drawer, next to the window wall, made of wood with a lock in it.

'If you have any valuables you're concerned about, you can keep them in that drawer or store them in the office safe. Your door can't be locked from the outside,' he told her, 'although you can lock it when you're inside.'

Haley wondered if he thought she needed that advice. She owned no

47

expensive jewelry, and, except for Roberta's necklace, had nothing of great value with her, but she nodded anyway.

After that, she didn't want to check her inexpensive watch to see the time, so she asked him instead.

'Four-thirty, Miss. We should begin to move very soon, so you may want to unpack before that. You can store your suitcase up there — ' He pointed to the space above the sink. ' — or I can store it for you in the baggage car.' He paused, and Haley wondered if he waited for a tip before leaving, but then she remembered the brochure had said all gratuities would be handled at the end of the tour.

Alan kept on talking. 'Reception in the Seattle car at five-thirty. Formal or informal — it's up to you.' He looked her over admiringly, as if picturing her in some slinky, figure-hugging evening gown.

'Thank you,' Haley said again, and this time she moved toward him, her hand stretched out to close the door. 'I'd better hurry and get changed then, hadn't I?'

'Oh, yes, Ma'am.' He backed out and Haley turned the lock. Well, she'd made one conquest already. Too bad he seemed about the age of her nephew.

★ ★ ★

Haley realized the brochure had been right when it said the closet in her cabin would be only four inches wide. However, thanks to the special tiered hangers she found inside, she hung a few dresses, skirts and pants within the space as well as from two hooks on the cabin's walls. She put her folded clothes in the plastic drawers, and — by standing on the side of the couch — managed to shove her empty suitcase onto the shelf above the sink. Finally, she stowed her billfold, cell phone and Roberta's necklace in the locked drawer, and put the key into her small evening purse.

After considerable deliberation, she decided to wear the black silk sheath, but, in her opinion, the low neckline revealed a lot of cleavage, and she tied her floral scarf over it and pinned it in place with a circular silver pin.

At five-thirty she entered the club car and moved slowly among the forty or more passengers who were already assembled in the car. People occupied every plush chair as well as the bench in front of the ebony baby grand piano, making it standing-room-only for her and several others.

She wove her way to the bar at the opposite end, accepted a filled champagne flute, then turned and inspected the passengers one at a time. The only young ones were a couple in the corner, and — judging by the way they held each other around the waist — honeymooners.

Haley maneuvered her way to the piano whose top contained a crisp white cloth, an enormous vase of red roses, several plates of hors d'oeuvres, and a small bowl of caviar. She helped herself to a cracker with cheese and nibbled on it while negotiating her way through the car. She saw some good-looking older men — forties to sixties — but invariably they wore wedding rings and/or a woman stood close by.

Roberta had given her a faint hope that something exciting would happen on the trip, but, at the moment, that seemed remote, and Haley let her anticipation return to normal. She would do just what she planned in the beginning — relax and learn about the South.

Then a large, husky young man entered and headed straight for the bar. Although no woman accompanied him, Haley dismissed him immediately as being too young — mid-twenties, she guessed — and not at all attractive. His face was round, his eyes small, and his ears stuck out. In addition, although the porter had said the reception would not be formal, this man had gone overboard in the opposite direction. He wore jeans that had seen better days and a dark green sport shirt. He looked straight at her and grinned before Haley realized she must have been staring, and she quickly turned her head.

Next, a tall, grey-haired man wearing a tuxedo came in, smiling and greeting people as he worked his way through the crowd. As if everyone realized his status, conversations gradually quieted and, from a position near the center of the room, he addressed the group.

'Good evening. I'm Walter Blaine and I represent the owners of the American Orient Express. We're very happy to have you aboard and hope you'll have a wonderful time.' He waited while people applauded.

'I'd especially like to welcome aboard a lady who has traveled with us before,' he said next, 'Mrs. Gertrude Draper.'

His gaze in Haley's direction made her face flush, then she realized he meant the woman sitting in one of the club chairs, and she saw the same woman who occupied the cabin next to hers. Mrs. Draper, her short gray hair neatly in place, wearing a simple black dress with a string of pearls at the neck, smiled but didn't rise. She seemed uncomfortable at being singled out.

'We hope all of you, like Mrs. Draper,' Blaine went on, 'will enjoy this trip so much you'll want to travel with us again in the future. And now,' he continued, 'I want to introduce you to one of the activities directors on this tour. Although you'll find an itinerary of each day's events in your cabins, I hope you'll feel free to ask him any questions you may have.'

He paused again before announcing, 'Here he is: Mr. Jonathan Shafer.'

5

Jon, too, wore a tuxedo and appeared as much at home in it as Cary Grant always did. He even walked a little like the actor, a kind of slow lope, his head level, never bouncing with his steps.

'Welcome,' he said, his voice carrying in the car. 'My name is Jonathan Shafer, but please call me Jon.'

He spoke for about ten minutes, describing the various side trips they'd be taking, then asked if there were any questions.

So, he was not a Mafia hit man, or even a wealthy business traveler, but an employee of the company. So much for fantasy. She felt guilty for a momentary snobbishness. Who was she, the next Grace Kelly? She was just a working girl and he was a working man.

She listened as someone asked about the fact that the train hadn't yet begun to move.

'It's the rain storm,' he answered. 'Four of our passengers were arriving in New Orleans this afternoon by plane and the storm has delayed their flight. As soon as they're on board, we'll be off.'

'Do you always hold up the train for latecomers?' someone else asked.

He grinned. 'We do our best to accommodate passengers who may be delayed, and, in this case, one of the delayed passengers is our piano player.'

He answered more questions, and after awhile, people began to get up and leave the car, seemingly toward one of the two dining cars. Haley headed in that direction as well.

She entered a room that seemed like something out of the past, almost as if she had boarded a train in Europe fifty years before. Lights in gleaming fixtures adorned the rich, dark wood on the sides of the car, casting a soft glow over tables — large enough for four people on one side of the car, for two on the other — covered in crisp white cloths. A small lamp sat on each table as well as shiny silver, crystal glassware, a vase with a fresh flower, and a printed menu in a blue leather folder.

Trying not to seem too dazzled by the splendor, Haley chose a seat at one of the smaller tables and opened the folder. Dinner, she saw, would be just as grand as everything else, consisting of five courses: appetizer, soup, salad, entree and dessert. Although the appetizer, soup and salad were already determined, she had her choice of four different main courses and five desserts. She found it hard to choose, but finally decided she'd skip the appetizer, have the salmon and chocolate torte.

She gave the waiter her order, admiring his navy blue jacket with the AOE logo.

'May I join you?'

Jon, who had apparently come up behind the waiter so she hadn't seen him, looked expectantly at her.

Her heart made a loop but she managed to say, 'Yes.'

He sat down and picked up the menu. 'Have you ordered?'

'Yes again.' She hadn't quite got over her surprise at discovering her assumptions about him had been wrong, but she was glad to let him share her table. She had always been an introvert, had difficulty making the first move when meeting people.

He smiled, then signaled to the waiter and ordered the exact dinner she had. Haley said nothing but wondered if he overheard and wanted to impress her, or if it was just a coincidence.

'I saw you leave the club car,' he said.

'I would have said, 'hello,' before I left, but you seemed engrossed in conversation with another passenger.'

'I had planned to suggest we dine together but it seems to have worked out that way after all.'

'You have a knack for saving me from having to eat dinner alone.'

'My pleasure.'

He fell silent, just gazed at her as if he hadn't really seen her closely before and wanted to commit her face to memory. She thought her face flushed and she glanced out the window, but could see nothing in the darkness.

She took a deep breath and looked back at him. 'So you're an activities director for the train.'

'I guess I owe you an apology. I should have told you that last night.'

'I got the impression you worked for a large corporation, one accustomed to expenses for fancy dinners in high-priced restaurants.'

The waiter put small soup tureens in front of them and Jon waited until he left before answering. 'I thought you wouldn't let me pay for your dinner otherwise.'

'So, no giant corporation is involved?'

'No, just your obedient servant. I hope you don't mind.'

'It does change things. I'm perfectly capable of paying for my own dinner. Unless, of course, the American Orient Express provided that as another passenger perk. How many of us get dinner at Antoine's?' She smiled. 'And the trip is only beginning.'

'It was my own idea, and I can afford it, even without an expense account.'

Suddenly the car jolted noisily, crystal glassware tinkled as it shook, and the train began to move. He glanced at his watch. 'Three hours late. I'm afraid our schedule is going to suffer.'

Haley spooned some of the clear broth. 'How long have you worked for the train company?'

'This is my first trip. I spent a few weeks in training — learning about the area we'll be visiting and the sights we'll be seeing — and we did a kind of shakedown run.'

'You sounded very knowledgeable in the club car.'

'I'm a quick study.'

They finished their soup and the handsome tureens were replaced with salad plates. 'I'm sorry if I misled you last night,' he added.

'My own fault, leaping to conclusions.' She decided to tell him the story.

'I have a good friend who insisted I would meet a — a wealthy man on this trip. So — '

'So that's where I came in?' He laughed, then said, 'You were hoping for a dot-com entrepreneur with a seven-figure income, not a working stiff.'

'My friend is an incurable romantic. She decided this would be another *North by Northwest*.'

' — one of my favorite films — '

' — and Cary Grant would come into the dining car — '

' — so you paid the waiter to seat me at your table.'

Haley laughed. 'It turned out not to be necessary.' She returned to her salad, wondering if she sounded too eager. Although he had explained a bit, he still seemed to wear an aura of mystery.

The salad plates were whisked away and dinner plates replaced them. The waiter poured wine into their glasses.

'Actually, I have a confession of my own to make,' Haley said. 'I'm not a professional model. Oh, I did some modeling in my teens, but I'm a schoolteacher, not, like Eva Marie Saint, a spy.'

He grinned. 'And I'm no movie star. So we're both just ordinary folks. Probably just as well. We wouldn't want to find ourselves having to fight a bunch of bad guys.'

She smiled back at him. 'If we don't, my friend will be disappointed. She wants me to have an adventure.'

'I'll do my best, but I'm afraid I can't guarantee anything more than a possibly rained-out excursion.'

'Possibly rained out? What do you mean?'

'The forecast for Jacksonville tomorrow is rain.'

'Well, I brought a raincoat.'

'That's the ticket,' he said, 'I like a woman who can take disaster in her stride.'

Haley hoped her face hadn't turned red. She felt ambivalent about his coming on to her. Just to please

Roberta, she had agreed to be a blonde on the train and to be open-minded about any eligible man she might meet. But in truth, she hadn't really expected it to happen. Yes, he was good looking and seemed very nice, but weren't things moving awfully fast? She wanted to slow down a bit, yet the trip would last only a week.

As she took a sip of wine, she looked at Jon over the rim of her glass. She'd be a fool to resist someone like him. And what harm could there be in a flirtation, especially since the 'flirtee' wasn't really her but this glamorous blonde? She'd try to just relax and enjoy whatever adventure came her way.

'So, tell me,' he asked, 'what do you teach?'

'History. I work for a private school and teach seventh graders. Next semester we're studying the Civil War, so this train trip seemed ideal.'

The waiter removed their plates and brought dessert.

Jon continued to study her. 'You're just taking this tour for educational purposes? It's not your vacation?'

'Can't I combine the two?'

'I guess so.' He tasted his torte. 'You teach history and you like old movies. Is there a connection there?'

'I haven't been psychoanalyzed, so I don't know why I love old things and old times, but I do.'

'Don't be ashamed of liking old movies. I like them too. I think it's great that, thanks to television and videos, we can still watch those wonderful old stars.'

'You probably like John Wayne — '

'Actually, I prefer Humphrey Bogart.'

'*The African Queen* is one of my favorites,' Haley said.

'Mine too. And how about those classics, *Casablanca* and *The Maltese Falcon*?'

The man was not only handsome, but a soulmate. After all, how many men liked those old movies? The male teachers at her school preferred films like *Armageddon* and *The Matrix*, full of noise and special effects. The very thought of having this in common with Jon made her self-conscious, as if he could see into her mind. And then that pessimism she often tried to squelch reared up and told her he probably didn't really like those old films at all, but just rattled off their titles to impress her. Not that it mattered, but she could ask questions, find out if he really knew all about them as she did.

But he changed the subject. 'Do you still model part-time, or do you have some other hobby for non-school hours?'

She felt disoriented for a moment before answering, wondered if she should even tell him. Some men were disturbed when she told them what she did in her spare time. But perhaps Jon would be different. Anyway, it didn't matter since, in six more days the tour would end and she would probably never see him again.

'I work at a shelter for battered and

abused women.'

He seemed puzzled rather than defensive. 'Really? Do you counsel them or — ?'

'No, I'm not a trained counselor. I just volunteer my time doing whatever is necessary to keep the place going.'

'Such as — ?'

'Most of my work involves doing the book-keeping and scheduling the volunteers who work at the used clothing store we maintain. Some of these women come in with nothing but the clothes on their backs, so the volunteers clean and repair donated clothes which we can give them.'

'Do the women stay in the shelter so long that you have to do that?'

'Sometimes. Every case is different.' She refolded her napkin again. 'Last year about eleven hundred women went through our shelter.'

'I'm surprised.'

'It's rewarding work, but depressing at times, not fun to talk about.' She hurried on. 'Besides I've talked too much about myself. What are your hobbies when you're not riding the rails?'

He took a sip of wine before answering. 'Just the usual guy stuff. I play a little golf, racquetball.'

'You said you'd just started this job. What did you do before?'

'You were right in your earlier guess. I did work for a large corporation, but I didn't like the atmosphere, people fighting for advantage, back-stabbing. Life is too short to live like that.'

Haley's opinion of him notched up a little more. She admired people who would rather not climb the corporate ladder by stepping on others' toes. 'Well, I hope you'll enjoy being activities director.'

'I like it already. Especially this part, getting to know you.'

Haley basked for a moment in his words, then changed the subject. 'I believe we're to have lunch in Jacksonville tomorrow.'

'Perhaps. Perhaps not.'

She glanced at him, felt her eyebrows rise.

'You see,' he said, 'we have an Amtrak engine and we travel on their tracks, but not the passenger tracks.'

'Then what kind?'

'Freight. That's why it's a little rough at times.'

'The movement seems quite smooth to me.'

'But that three-hour delay getting started might mean that we miss our window to get through certain areas tonight. And, since freight has the right of way, that means we could be shunted off to a siding until the freight cars go through.'

'And then — ' she prompted.

'More delays. We might not arrive in Jacksonville in time for the side trip.' He grinned. 'I probably shouldn't be telling you this.'

'You mean the company wouldn't like it? But it's not like the airlines, who sometimes keep you in the dark about flight delays. I think they do that so the passengers can't book a seat on a different airline.'

'You may be right.'

'But we can't take a different train even if we wanted to. This trip is like a cruise on land. We signed up for the whole thing, not just getting from point A to point B.'

'That's very understanding of you.'

'So long as I end up in Washington next Friday.' She watched as the waiter poured coffee into their cups. 'Well, actually Saturday is okay too. I'd still get home in time to teach school on Monday morning.'

'So this is your spring break?'

'Yes. And what will you do after the train arrives in Washington?'

'Take the afternoon off and show up again the next morning to do the same trip in reverse. Back to New Orleans.'

'And will you do that all year?'

'Oh, no. After that the train begins to go west.'

'I remember the brochure mentioned some other trips. Will you go on those?'

'Perhaps.'

'You're not sure?'

He frowned. 'I'm a little undecided about my next move.' He got up and came around to help her from her chair. 'Why don't we go into the club car and listen to the music for awhile?'

As they walked gingerly through the two dining cars toward the second club car, Haley pondered Jon's last remark. He'd become mysterious once again. He had only taken this job within the past few weeks, and now he seemed to be thinking of ditching it already. What else would he do? If he disliked the corporate rat-race, what else could he do? She knew little about him and her normal instinct told her not to get involved. But, she reminded herself, she had no intention of getting *really* involved. This vacation would help her learn about the south for her students, but the nights were for having fun, and she had promised Roberta to do just that.

The piano player — an attractive fortyish woman with short blonde hair and a strong, melodious voice — sang old standards and Haley and Jon joined three other passengers around the piano. Haley began to sing the words to one of the songs.

'Louder,' he said.

Haley felt herself flush. Always a wallflower, she never wanted the spotlight. But now — tonight, in a blonde wig, on this glamorous train, with Jon beside her . . .

When the number ended, John said, 'You like old songs too?'

'Yes, my mother worked when I was growing up and my sister and I stayed with our grandmother. She played her old albums every day.'

'I like the music of the forties and fifties myself.'

'Those tunes are as familiar to me as anything being sung these days by Norah Jones or Mariah Carey.'

'Who?' Jon asked, and they laughed. He refused to chime in on the next one however, saying he had a voice like a rusty hinge.

He stood at her side, watching her, smiling at the others around the piano, and she found herself enjoying the camaraderie of the group.

Finally, the crowd in the club car began to thin out and she glanced at her watch. 'It's later than I thought.'

'Let me walk you back to your cabin,' Jon said.

Each time they came to the heavy doors between cars, he sprang ahead and opened them for her, then reminded her to be careful crossing from one moving car to the other. He took her arm to steady her against the swaying and jolting of the car over the tracks.

'Do you have your own compartment?' she asked him.

'The crew has a sleeping car up front, right behind the one with the washing machines that run all night.'

'I'll bet you don't hear them,' she said. 'At least not while the train is moving.'

'I'll find out, won't I?' At her

compartment, he said good night and held her hand for a long moment.

Haley pulled away as gracefully as she could, but then he put his arms around her and kissed her firmly. She couldn't remember the last time a man had kissed her. How wonderful it felt, those warm lips on hers, the pressure of his mouth, the feel of his long lean body against hers. She wanted it to last longer, but he said good night again, turned and left.

She pushed into the room and closed the door slowly, leaned against it for a moment, wondering if he'd felt as lightheaded as she did. But should she have let him kiss her? That evening had been a kind of second date, and men generally expected some indication of how a woman felt by that time. She liked him and apparently they both knew it. If only he didn't seem mysterious at times.

She sighed, then noticed the couch had been made up into a bed already, with white sheets, a woolen blanket, fat pillow with a mint in silver paper on it, and a printed itinerary of the next days' activities, complete with expected weather report. She put the latter into the expandable pocket under the window and pulled down the shade.

Undressing proved to be much more difficult than dressing had been. The train seemed to be going very fast over a winding stretch of track and she kept losing her balance and bumping into the walls. She pulled off her wig and stored it in the expandable pouch on the wall, put her scarf in one of the plastic drawers under the bed, then removed her dress and hung it on the back of the lavatory door. Brushing her teeth proved challenging as well, and then she began to wonder if the train's motion would keep her awake. Had this been a big mistake? Could she get seasick on a train or would the rocking put her to sleep? She hoped the latter would be true. In any event, she couldn't back out now.

She searched the other drawer for her

night-gown, then had an idea. Rather than compete with others wanting to use the shower room in the morning, she'd take her shower that night. She pulled on the robe, stepped into her slippers and peeked out the door.

In the dimly lighted corridor she saw and heard no one. At the end of the car, she opened the door marked 'Shower' and found there were actually two little rooms. The first had a bench, several large white towels on rods and hooks on which to hang her robe. She locked the door, took off the robe, and turned to the other room, lined in stainless steel with a drain in the floor. She stepped inside, pulled the shower curtain closed and turned the knobs, letting hot water flow over her body.

She scrubbed the make-up from her face and even shampooed her hair, knowing that, since her forced haircut, it would dry quickly. Toweled off, back in the terry robe, she opened the door and stepped into the corridor. Only to be met by a man just coming into the car. She nearly choked. He was the last person in the world she wanted to see at that moment.

Jon.

6

What on earth was Jonathan Shafer doing in the corridor of the Istanbul sleeping car at that time of night? He had left her there about an hour before, after telling her his own compartment was at the front of the train. His duties as activity director surely didn't include checking the sleeping cars. Or was he spying on her?

She shuddered. There she was in the corridor, wearing nothing but a terry robe, *sans* wig. How would she ever explain why she suddenly had no long blonde hair, but these very short, damp, brown curls? Her throat dried up at the very thought. And, with him blocking the narrow passage, she could not escape. She shrank back against the wall away from the dim light in the corner. Maybe he wouldn't see her. Maybe he'd just go on through, perhaps to the observation car for a nightcap.

But, no, he saw her. 'Well, hi,' he said.

She didn't answer, couldn't answer. Her tongue felt thick in her mouth. All she could think of was that she would kill Roberta when she got home, because Roberta had insisted on the wig and now she was caught without it and about to look like a fool.

'You look familiar. Have we met?'

Haley pulled the collar of the robe up to her chin and tried to squeeze her face into it. 'No, I don't think so.'

Jon smiled. 'I'm Jonathan Shafer, one of the activities directors. How do you do?'

Omigod. Was it possible he didn't recognize her? Of course. Without the wig and make-up — to say nothing of clothes — he wouldn't. She'd learned long ago that men were not that observant, except about football games.

'Hi,' she said. She hoped the one syllable wouldn't give her away.

'Excuse me. This isn't the best time

to make your acquaintance, but I thought I'd met everyone in this car.' He paused as if waiting for her to give her name, but she said nothing. 'Are you traveling alone?'

She raised her voice above its normal level and said, 'Yes.' It sounded like a squeak. Why didn't he take a hint and go away? He was striking up a conversation with a woman who just got out of the shower! Friendliness was one thing, but really!

'Well, I hope to see you again.' Still he stood in her way, grinning like a Cheshire cat.

She had no room to maneuver past him but, even if she did, and he watched her return to her compartment, he'd know who she was. She had no choice but to wait him out. She shrank back further into the shadows.

'Oh, I'm keeping you. Sorry.' Finally he made a move to go, then turned to her again. 'Good night.'

Again using a high-pitched voice she said, 'Good night,' as well.

With a last glance back, he made his way down the corridor, but Haley didn't leave her spot near the shower room until he reached the other end of the car and she heard the door open and close. Then she dashed into her compartment.

Safely inside, she turned the lock in the door and leaned against the bed. What luck. He hadn't recognized her. She hung up the robe and pulled on her nightgown, then brushed her teeth, switched off the light and crawled into bed. But something nagged at her mind. Oh, yes, hadn't he been awfully friendly with the person he thought she was? Had he been coming on to *her*? True, she no longer looked like her head had been in a chopping machine. It had been over a week and her hair grew fast. But was he the kind of man who would make up to any young woman on the train? Especially after he had just kissed *her*?

She felt her stomach give a little lurch. So, she wasn't the only woman he was attracted to. The fact that the other woman was also her didn't alter the fact that he had flirted — albeit briefly — with her. All evening he had acted as if she was the most exciting woman he'd ever seen, never leaving her side. And then he'd been almost as attentive to *her*. She was her own rival.

It was really sort of funny. The comic element in the episode took over her thoughts and she grinned in the dark. It would be an amusing story to tell Roberta when she got home. She turned on her side and soon fell asleep.

* * *

Jon continued down the corridor, left the Istanbul car, then went through the Berlin car, headed for Observation. His thoughts, however, remained on Haley. So his suspicions were correct: she wore a blonde wig. Why did she feel the need to cover her own short, brown hair? And why hadn't she corrected him when he pretended he didn't recognize her, that they'd never met?

Okay, the wig was sort of glamorous in a Hollywood way, but she needn't try to look like Gwyneth Paltrow or any other movie star for his benefit. She was quite attractive even without the wig. Especially without the wig. That short curly hair suited her pixie face, her eyes were an unusual shade of blue-green, and she looked just fine without make-up.

He also admired her figure, and although he hadn't seen it just then — covered up as it was in the terry robe — he'd noticed the curves in all the right places during dinner, thanks to the dress she wore. He suspected she used the scarf to cover the neckline which dipped low in front, but the scarf shifted from time to time as she moved, revealing an enticing hint of cleavage.

As for her pretending they'd never met, that was okay with him. He could go along with a gag. A woman with a sense of humor always rated a plus. There were far too few of them to suit him. Not that he needed a lot of women in his life. One would do very well, thank you. It was time to think of settling down again and right from the first, he'd had a good feeling about Haley Parsons.

Too bad he couldn't spend more time with her, but he was supposed to be figuring out if someone was stealing from the passengers. On the previous trip that season, both a valuable bracelet and expensive brooch had been reported stolen and, if possible, he needed to find out who had done it and keep it from happening again.

He'd checked the employment records of every staff member on board and — as time and their duties permitted — he would interview them. So far his investigation had netted him only two possible suspects: Miguel — the bartender in the observation car — and Tom Smith, the laundry worker who'd been hired at the last minute before the trip started, because the original hiree hadn't shown up.

Miguel looked like the Hispanic he was: dark-haired, brown-eyed. He was slender and agile, and when he spoke — which was seldom — it was with an accent. He hadn't made friends with any other crew members — a loner — and seemed very subdued, even mysterious. Still, to be fair, a quiet person shouldn't be considered suspicious for that reason alone.

Smith was just the opposite, fair-skinned with blond hair and quite tall. Of course, his size didn't make him suspicious, anything but. A tall person tended to be remembered. In Jon's experience, con men and thieves wanted to be as inconspicuous as possible. Short, wiry, nondescript men were more successful at evading detection because they weren't distinctive or memorable. That could be useful in a line-up.

No, what had attracted Jon's attention to Smith was his attitude. Something about him seemed to hint he had more on his mind than tending industrial-sized washing machines and scrubbing kitchens in the dining cars. And then there was that phone call. He'd stepped off the train when he should have been on the job, and made a call on a cell phone. One of the porters spotted him five yards away, seemingly hiding behind a building, and reported it. But Smith hadn't been on the previous trip, so he couldn't have been the thief.

On the other hand, Miguel had also made a call, using a pay phone when the train was stopped. But, hell, what was mysterious about making calls? Everyone had a life outside the train and friends or family to keep in touch with. Maybe it wasn't either of those guys. Maybe, in fact, it was Haley.

Had she been a passenger on the earlier trip — possibly under a different name — and this time wore a wig to change her appearance?

He sighed. His assignment wasn't going to be easy. But he hoped the guilty person wouldn't turn out to be Haley Parsons.

7

Haley woke to see dim light creeping in around the drawn shade. Had the light wakened her, or was it the fact that the train wasn't moving? She glanced at her watch and decided it wasn't too early to go to the dining car for breakfast. But after dressing in pants and blouse in a shade of blue-green that Roberta had insisted matched Haley's eyes, she rolled up the window shade only to discover that outside the sky was overcast and rain still fell in sheets.

She'd slept wonderfully, the motion of the train rocking her to sleep, but she was grateful it had stopped for the moment so she could apply make-up without danger of smearing it all over her face. Once more wearing the blonde wig, as well as a long-sleeved sweater against the look of the weather out-doors, she entered the corridor and turned right. Although the train wasn't moving, she had a clear vision of which was forward and which was back. In a way that was strange because normally she considered herself directionally-impaired and, without a map, couldn't find her way home from a strange part of her own town.

As she passed through the next sleeping car and the Seattle Club car, she wondered if she'd see Jon that morning, but when she entered the dining car, she cast her gaze around to no avail. Mixed emotions tumbled about in her mind. On one hand she wanted to spend more time with him. On the other, she felt doing so might be unwise. After all, he had flirted with two women on the train. True, both of them were her, but he didn't know that.

She would have chosen a seat at an empty table for two, as she had the night before, but, seeing the Jacksons, who also had a cabin in her car, at one of the larger tables, she asked if she might join them instead.

A momentary feeling of panic clutched her. She never made new friends easily. What if they said no, that they were waiting for someone else? Was it the blonde wig and the expensive clothes making her bold? But then Mrs. Jackson smiled, Mr. Jackson rose and pulled out a chair for her, and Haley relaxed.

Although they were older than Haley — in their fifties, she supposed — they found much in common and chatted easily over breakfast. Leaving the table finally, she returned to her cabin, but her porter, Alan, had not quite finished restoring the bed to its status as a couch. While waiting, she decided to check out the rest of the train. The observation car, she'd been told, served a continental breakfast and, entering, the strong aroma of freshly-brewed coffee met her, and she decided to have a second cup. One end of the polished wooden bar held platters of sliced fresh fruit and trays of muffins, breads and rolls, and they looked so appetizing, Haley decided she'd have breakfast there another time. The uniformed bartender — a handsome man with thick black hair and mustache, whose name tag indicated he was Miguel — poured her coffee and she took it to the coffee table fronting one of the sofas.

About ten other passengers sat on the plush chairs and sofas in the car, also enjoying fruit and rolls and drinking coffee, a few of them talking in low tones. But none of them was Jon. Her sensible side told her she shouldn't keep thinking about him because, other considerations aside, the trip would soon be over and they'd part anyway. In the meantime, she didn't want either of them to get hurt. She sighed and settled into her seat.

She looked out the wide windows to see the train was stopped in the proverbial middle of nowhere, with only empty fields with large buildings — that might be industrial warehouses — in the distance. Miguel came over with a pot of coffee and asked if she'd like a refill. As he poured, she realized she had seen him the night before and not in the observation car. But while she tried to remember where, the train made a noisy jolt, the coffee sloshed in her cup and they began to move.

After awhile, she took her coffee to the cushioned seat at the rear of the car and watched the rails slip away behind the train. The rain blurred everything — trees, buildings, houses — to a montage of gray and brown. Not exactly the sunny South.

Restless, she returned to her carriage, but the thought of staying in her compartment bored her. She headed for the Seattle club car and found a few people there reading newspapers. Four passengers had taken over the card table and were playing Bridge, so she browsed among the shelves of books in the corner looking for something about the history of the South. But the one she finally found turned out to be about southern cooking and she closed it with a sigh. She dubbed her own culinary efforts *Cordon Noir* because, unless Roberta was there to check up on her, she invariably burned something.

She moved to one of the upholstered swivel chairs and stared out at the gray and sullen weather outside the windows, listening to the clack-clack of the train wheels. After awhile, Walter Blaine came through the car announcing that since they had not yet arrived in Jacksonville, lunch would be served on board, and Haley decided she'd stay in the club car where sandwiches were provided. She wasn't very hungry, anyway. It seemed only moments since she'd had breakfast.

Again, in spite of herself, she thought about Jon. She wanted to talk to him, watch his firm smooth lips when he spoke, look into his Paul Newman blue eyes. She had finally met a man who excited her, and she wanted to spend every minute of those few days she would have with him. The little voice of wisdom that usually kept her from doing the wrong thing told her she was playing with fire. Roberta had been right in predicting she'd meet a

handsome, single man, but, clairvoy-
ance notwithstanding, she wasn't going
to fall in love with him nor he with her.
That sort of thing only happened in
movies. And, besides, he had no serious
interest in her. Sure, he'd kissed her,
but some men kissed women as a
matter of habit, or just to show they
could. If that kiss really meant he cared,
he'd have been around to see her this
morning, wouldn't he?

An hour later, as she started to eat a
turkey and swiss cheese sandwich, she
looked up and saw Jon come in. He sat
down beside her.

'I'm so glad to see you,' they said in
unison, and then laughed.

'You first,' Haley said. Her heart raced
and she wished she hadn't blurted out
her thoughts like that.

'I wanted to have breakfast with you,
but I've been busy. Had to do some
work, you know. I see I'm too late for
lunch.'

'Not if you just want a sandwich.'

He got up, helped himself to one

from the tray on the top of the piano and returned to her side. 'Did you sleep well last night?'

'Yes, very well.'

'Traveling over the rough roadbed didn't disturb you?'

'I think all the rocking put me to sleep.'

While they ate, she thought of his attention to the 'strange' woman he met coming out of the shower the night before, and would have liked to bring up the subject just to learn how he'd handle it, but of course she couldn't without revealing she, herself, was the object of his advances.

Well, perhaps advances was too strong a word. After all, he was an activities director. It was probably his job to be sure every passenger had a good time. And being especially friendly to women traveling alone might be required. She supposed it was similar to the practice she'd heard about cruise ships — that they hired unattached men to be available to dance on board in the evenings with single women.

'I enjoyed our dinner,' Jon said then, 'and the fact you like old movies too. Most of the single women I've met haven't seen anything older than *Harry Potter*.'

Haley remembered their conversation and wondered if he'd been serious. Did he really like them or did he only say that to impress her? She decided the reason didn't matter, but she asked anyway. 'How is it you happen to like old movies?'

'After my divorce — and because of a job I held at the time — I spent a lot of nights alone, sometimes in hotel rooms, and television was my only entertainment.'

That sounded plausible, and for a moment she felt sorry for him, imagining lonely nights with nothing but now-deceased actors as company. 'Which do you like best, *Casablanca* or *The Maltese Falcon*?'

'They're both great, but I think I like *The Maltese Falcon* a bit better. The last scene is a classic, of course, when Bogey tells Mary Astor he's sending her over, but I also like his disarming Elijah Wood and humiliating him in front of Sidney Greenstreet.'

So he did know the movie. Not only that, he shared her opinion of which was better.

After another pause, in which he seemed to be searching his memory, he said, 'Did you ever see *Three Strangers* with Greenstreet and Peter Lorre?'

'Of course.' Haley felt as if bees had taken up residence in her midriff. He knew *Three Strangers*! None of her friends — not even Roberta who had come to like the old films because of Haley — had ever heard of the black and white thriller, and it was one of her favorites.

Finished with his sandwich, Jon crossed his legs and settled himself more deeply in the short sofa. 'We need more films like those, don't we?'

'I wish I had lived when they were making them,' Haley said. 'I'm sure there are dozens more that are every bit as good but were never saved.'

'You wouldn't really want to live back then, would you?' he asked.

'Oh yes. The world was a better place. For one thing, there were far fewer people then.' She warmed to her topic. 'Every place is crowded now, traffic is impossible, the air and water are polluted, they're cutting down forests. Politicians care only about the next election and businessmen are even worse, taking huge salaries and stock options while . . . '

'Whoa,' Jon said. 'What brought all this on?'

Haley felt her face flush. 'Sorry. But you did ask, didn't you?'

'Don't you think you're being a little too hard on the present?'

'Not really. I'd give up all the so-called modern conveniences if we could go back to living the way they did in the forties and fifties.'

He grinned. 'I think you've been watching *too many* old movies.'

So he didn't agree with her. Few people did and she was used to indulgent smiles from the majority. She was disappointed that Jon, who agreed with her about movies, however, didn't share her feelings about the problems of the twenty-first century. On the other hand, since theirs would never be a long-term relationship, perhaps it really didn't matter.

His pager went off. 'Excuse me, I'm going to have to check in at the office.' He squeezed her hand. 'See you later.'

Haley got up, returned their two plates to the bartender and left the car. As she moved through the train cars to her own cabin, she thought about the conversation she'd just had with Jon. She shouldn't have been so vocal about her opinions. Most people — especially men — didn't agree with her, and perhaps that's what had frightened them away on the few occasions when she did have a date. Would she never learn?

Frustrated with her poor social skills, she decided to tidy the drawers in which she'd thrown her clothes the night before. She refolded the print scarf she'd worn, but couldn't find the silver pin that had held it in place. She searched both plastic drawers without success, then the locked drawer, although she was sure she hadn't put it there. She also looked in the expandable pockets on the wall under the window and in the lavatory, then got down on her knees to check the floor. Nothing. Had she taken it off the night before, or had she lost the pin in the dining room or club car and never noticed? Well, if she had dropped it somewhere, there was one way to find out.

She negotiated the swaying carriages toward the office at the end of the club car and approached the window. Inside, she could see a tiny room crammed with files, computers, printers, and other equipment. A young red-haired woman sat at a narrow desk and, when she saw Haley, put aside the papers in front of her. 'What can I do for you?'

'I seem to be missing a piece of jewelry,' Haley said.

The woman's smile turned into a frown. 'What kind of jewelry?'

'A silver pin.' She gestured with her hands. 'It's round, plain. In fact, it's not very valuable, but I can't find it in my compartment and I wondered if I might have dropped it somewhere in the train and someone — perhaps a porter or waiter — might have found it.'

'Nothing has been turned in,' the woman said, 'and the carpets have been vacuumed already.'

Haley shrugged, said, 'Thanks anyway,' and turned to go.

The redhead stopped her. 'Just a minute. I want you to talk to someone else about it.' She picked up a portable phone and punched in some numbers.

'Really,' Haley protested, 'it's not that important.'

'It is to us.' After a moment she spoke to someone and then closed the phone and looked up at Haley again. 'He'll be right here. Please wait.'

Haley didn't know who 'he' was, but gave her a smile of appreciation, amazed at what lengths the company would go to over such a small thing. Suddenly Jon entered the car and, with only a brief glance in her direction, hurried up to the office. Haley moved out of his way so he could talk to the girl inside.

Jon leaned into the window. 'What is it?'

'A missing piece of jewelry.' The young woman signaled for Haley to come near. 'This is Jon Shafer. He's in charge of security.'

Haley did a double-take. Jonathan Shafer in charge of security? Not an activities director? Or did he do both? The man was everything and everywhere. First he had been the one with a reservation at Antoine's, then he was introduced as an activities director and invited himself to her table at dinner the night before, and now he was suddenly in charge of security and apparently supposed to help her find her missing pin. There was no escaping him.

It seemed Fate, an apparent ally of Roberta, was conspiring to make him a part of her life.

8

Jon turned to her, genuine concern etched on his face. 'You've lost some jewelry?'

'Just a small silver pin. Nothing major. It wasn't expensive.'

'Let's go where we can talk about it.' He took her elbow, his touch sending warm sensations shooting up her arm and through her body, but — due to the narrowness of the hallway — he dropped it soon enough and guided her toward the main part of the car. Few people occupied the chairs, and Jon stopped about halfway, paused in front of one of the sofas, and motioned for her to take a seat.

'It's really not that important,' she protested. She continued to stand, still confused at his constantly changing occupations. 'Just costume jewelry. I wouldn't even have mentioned it, but I thought I might have dropped it somewhere and someone turned it in.'

'Please sit here,' he insisted. She did.

'Now,' he said, settling himself beside her, 'let's have the details.'

'I keep telling you, it's really nothing.'

'I'll be the judge of that. Describe the pin to me, please.'

'Smaller than a coaster, flat, silver.' Once again, she tried to describe it with her hands.

'Solid?'

'No, open in the center, like a circle.' She paused. 'I wore it last night. Do you remember seeing it?'

He rubbed his chin. 'As a matter of fact, I do. When did you see it last?'

'I'm not sure. I used it to hold my scarf in place but I really don't remember taking it off when I undressed to go to bed. The train was shaking so much at that time, I was just happy to get my clothes put away without falling down.' She glanced up at the passing scenery. 'Not like now. It's very smooth at the moment.'

'Yes, I remember it was pretty bumpy for awhile. Anyway, when did you realize the pin was gone?'

'Just a few minutes ago. After you left the club car, I decided to straighten my clothes in the drawers — I'd just sort of thrown them in last night — and I noticed the scarf was there, but not the pin.'

'And you didn't remember taking it off and putting it somewhere else?'

'I looked everywhere else, just in case.'

He frowned. 'Do you mind if we go to your compartment and look again? Just to be sure,' he added.

'No, I don't mind.'

They got up and returned to her cabin, Jon again opening the doors between the cars for her. Once inside the cabin, she pulled out the first plastic drawer and removed the garments one by one, placing them on the couch until the drawer was empty. No pin, just blouses, sweaters, pants that couldn't fit into the closet, but Jon checked each item, making sure the pin wasn't caught on something. The way he touched her clothes seemed suddenly erotic, as if he were caressing the woman who had worn them. She felt her face flush.

The second drawer contained her underwear and, as she removed nylon bras, panties and slips, her throat constricted. This time, she was the one to run her hands over them to be sure the pin wasn't attached. The mere thought of him handling her underwear made her entire body hot. But there was no pin there either.

Next she unlocked the wooden drawer and removed her purse, cell phone, travelers checks, and the long, blue velvet box containing Roberta's necklace. She opened the lid of the box to show Jon.

'This is the only expensive jewelry I have, and it's not even mine. My friend Roberta lent it to me.' She also pulled out the small cloth bag containing her other few pieces of jewelry: a twisted silver chain and a small strand of pearls.

Jon felt around in the empty drawer, then watched her replace the items. 'You really ought to put that necklace in the office safe when you're not wearing it. And the other jewelry, for that matter.'

'I suppose you're right.' But she relocked the drawer and put the key in her pocket.

Next he searched the expandable pouch under the window as well as the one in the lavatory. He peered closely at the floors, commenting that they'd been vacuumed when the porter made up the bed that morning, and checked the tiny sink and its holders for bottled water and her glass and toothpaste. Finally he looked up at her suitcase on the shelf above.

'Did you put the pin in your suitcase by any chance?'

'No, I'm sure of that. I wasn't about to try to get that up and down last night while the train was moving.'

Besides, why would she put it there when she might want to wear it again?

That would be almost as inconvenient as putting it in the office safe. 'There's nothing in the suitcase except those cotton sock things I put my shoes in when I pack.'

Jon stared around the room again, seemingly examining the very walls for clues to the pin's whereabouts. 'Pockets?'

'My rain coat has pockets, but of course I didn't wear it last night.'

Nevertheless, Jon pulled out the hangers from the tiny closet and let her search every pocket. Then he inspected her shoes, shoving his hand inside each one and even shaking them. Finally, he checked the pocket of the terry cloth robe. Also to no avail.

'I think you're right. It's not here.'

Haley had another idea. 'Could it have fallen down between the cushions?'

'The porter would have found it there when he made up the bed.' Even so, he ran his hands behind the couch as far as they would go.

At that moment, the train made a sharp turn and Haley lost her balance and fell against him. He held her tightly for a moment, his arm around her waist, and she smelled his aftershave and the clean laundry-scent of his white shirt under the blazer. How long had it been since a man held her so tightly? The feeling made her giddy. Then she pulled away, embarrassed.

'Not much space in here,' she said, looking at the floor instead of him. Her body felt warm and tingly, telling her not to be so hasty, that she'd like to have a fling, even a very brief one. She'd promised Roberta she was agreeable to a vacation romance. After all, other people did it all the time.

Jon, too, seemed affected by her moment in his arms. She thought she detected a flush creeping up his face. Then he backed away toward the door. 'Let's go back to the club car,' he suggested, 'and talk about this.'

'There's nothing to talk about. The pin is lost and maybe someone will turn it in later. No big deal.'

'No, I need to tell you something.' He opened the door and gently pulled her through, then pointed her back down the corridor in the direction from which they'd come.

This time, before sitting down in the club car, he said, 'Let me get us some tea. Or would you prefer coffee?'

'Tea is fine.'

He strolled to the bar where an ever-present bartender reached under the counter to come up with cups into which he poured hot water from a carafe.

Jon brought them back, along with sugar and tea, on a small tray, and Haley opened a packet of Constant Comment and put the tea bag and some sugar into her cup.

'You're making a mountain out of a mole-hill,' she said.

'No, I'm not and, although perhaps I shouldn't, I'll tell you why.' He took a long swallow of his tea, then returned the cup to its saucer and settled deeply into the corner of the sofa, turning slightly so he almost completely faced her. 'This isn't the first time a piece of jewelry has gone missing.'

'What?' Her voice rose.

He lowered his. 'Not so loud. We don't need to tell everyone.'

No one else sat near them but Haley leaned toward him and spoke almost in a whisper. 'Are you saying that jewelry has been lost on this train before?'

'Not this particular trip, at least not so far as I know. Yours may be the first.'

'Then when?'

'On the run before this, two passengers complained about lost jewelry. We tell them to lock it up or put it in the office safe, but people grow careless after a few days on board.'

'Where did they lose it?'

'From their rooms.'

'Then it was stolen?'

'Missing, not necessarily stolen. They aren't always sure where they saw it last. Like you,' he added. 'For all we know, it turned up later in their luggage.'

'But if it was stolen, can they sue the train owners?'

'No one has, so far, and in nine years it's never happened before, but it's obviously not a good thing for their image.'

'But how can they stop it?'

He took another sip of tea and she answered for him. 'That's why you're here. Because you're . . . ?'

'They've asked me to see if I could find out what's going on. If it was anything but a one-time occurrence.'

'Why you? Do activities directors normally do double duty as security guards?'

'They tell everyone I'm an activities director, but I'm really on board to keep an eye out for a possible thief.'

'A thief,' she repeated. 'One of the passengers?'

'More likely a member of the crew. After all, they have access to all the rooms and have the best chance to get away with something like this.'

'Aren't they screened thoroughly

before they're hired?'

'Of course, but some people can't resist temptation. If it looks easy, they may try to get away with it.'

'And apparently someone has already.'

'Perhaps. Remember, although the company pays the crew pretty good wages, it's obvious they aren't as well off as the passengers. This is a luxury train, and passengers generally have more than average incomes. Those people are hardly likely to need to steal jewelry from someone else.'

'I guess that makes sense.' She remembered something else he'd said. 'But, why you?'

'Because I once worked for the F.B.I.'

'You were a spy?' This was getting to be more like *North by Northwest* all the time, only he was the spy instead of her.

'No, the F.B.I., not the C.I.A. I just understand investigation techniques, and they could be sure I'd be discreet.'

'Let me get this straight. You're not an activities director for the train.

You're a security guard?'

'An investigator.'

Haley let out the breath she didn't realize she'd been holding. She brought her cup to her lips with both hands and took another sip of tea while she adjusted her image of him for the second time. Just when she was thinking she had him figured out, he had changed like a chameleon once more. He was no wealthy businessman, and no activities director. He'd once been in the F.B.I, but now he wasn't. Actually, except for being a temporary security guard, little more than a night watchman, he didn't have a job at all!

*　*　*

Jon studied her face over the rim of his cup. She was attractive even when she frowned. And these short sofas — didn't they call them love seats? — brought her so close to him, he could smell her perfume and the orange-sweet smell of her breath. The memory of touching her clothes, looking at her underwear and nightgown, to say nothing of holding her in his arms when the train made that sudden turn, were making him uncomfortable right now. He set his cup down, leaned back and balanced his right ankle on his other knee.

One thing was clear, however. She wasn't the train bandit he was sent to look for. Okay, she wore a blonde wig, and he still didn't know why, but she wouldn't have reported her pin missing if she was the thief. That relieved his doubts and he could concentrate on the two guys he thought most likely. Also, he could pursue Haley Parsons with lust, instead of detection, on his mind.

9

Haley sighed. 'What do we do now?'

'What I'd like you to do is keep your eyes and ears open and let me know if you notice anything the least bit suspicious.' He paused. 'Naturally, I'll be doing the same thing myself, trying to find out who's responsible.'

'Do you suspect anyone?'

'As I said, a member of the crew is most likely to be the thief, if there is a thief.'

'My porter perhaps?'

'Perhaps.'

'But Alan is such a nice, clean-cut looking young man. I find it hard to imagine him stealing anything.' Yes, he'd spent an exceptionally long time cleaning her cabin that morning, but she dismissed that as hardly being suspicious.

'You can never be sure about people.

Con men are notorious for looking like the last person in the world you'd suspect.'

'I suppose you're right. My mother once typed resumes for a college kid and he offered to sell her a typewriter that turned out to be stolen.'

'Did your mother get into trouble? Accepting stolen property is a crime too, you know.'

'No, fortunately, she didn't accept the typewriter, but a friend of hers did and they couldn't believe he'd stolen it. He was a short, skinny kid with glasses and looked like your average computer nerd.'

'Well, keep a sharp lookout and I'll do the same.'

Haley thought of the previous night when Jon had come into her sleeping car just as she came out of the shower. Was he prowling the car looking for anything suspicious about Alan then? No, he couldn't be. At that point she hadn't reported the pin missing. But she didn't bring up the fact that she'd seen Jon when she came out of the shower the night before.

'Probably there's nothing to worry about,' Jon said next, apparently trying to ease her mind. 'Maybe those other losses weren't thefts at all, and those passengers found the items later. Maybe someone found your pin and just hasn't turned it in yet.' He grinned. 'Or maybe it's just one of those mysterious disappearances that sometimes happen.'

'Like socks that vanish in the clothes dryer.'

'Right.' He laughed, a deep chuckle that would be fatherly if his voice weren't so sexy.

She had to rein in her thoughts. This was a vacation, not a husband-hunting expedition. They were only — how did that saying go — ships that pass in the night. Nothing would — could — come of their meeting. She never knew anyone who met her husband on a vacation. Maybe it could happen, but, in her experience, they invariably married the guy next door, a high school or college classmate or someone they met at work. She was only willing to have a mild flirtation, not commit herself for life.

'Tell me more about yourself,' he said, making her feel as if he had just read her mind.

'I'm afraid I did all the talking last night.'

'Not really. All I know is that you teach history at a private school. And that you like old movies and know the words to old songs.' He paused. 'Oh yes, and that you wish you'd lived fifty years ago, which, incidentally, I don't believe.'

'No, it's true. I've always preferred the past. Roberta laughs, but she knows I mean it when I said I should have been born a generation or two earlier.'

'You look like a modern woman to me. What's your hang-up?'

Haley struggled with herself. Only an hour before, she'd told herself to stop bringing up the past or she'd scare Jon away as she had everyone else, but he seemed so interested, a fellow believer, perhaps.

She plunged ahead, letting the chips fall where they might. 'I don't like what I see happening in the world — or at least in the United States — these days.'

'Aside from the things you mentioned before, what makes you say that?'

'Well, since I teach school, the most obvious is what's come to be called 'the dumbing down of America.' Children — even teens — can't spell and their grammar is atrocious. Every semester students show up in my classes knowing less than the group before.'

'They just know more about different things, I guess, like computers and the Internet.'

'Late night talk show hosts ask people — some of them college students — basic questions and they haven't a clue. One thought the Civil War occurred in the twentieth century. Another didn't know what country we fought during the War of 1812.'

'I guess that's why they need teachers like you.'

'I'm only one person. I feel as if I'm manning the trenches all alone.' She felt her face grow warm again. In a way it was her chance to talk to someone who was not another teacher and explain what was wrong with the world as she saw it.

'When my mother went to school, the worst things children did was chew gum in class, run through the halls and play hooky. Now they use illegal drugs, and too many young girls get pregnant.'

'Oh, come on,' Jon said, 'experimenting with adult behavior has always been a part of teen-age life.'

'Maybe so, but it was hidden. At least, it seems to have been. My mother told me that, when she was young, families were like those old television shows: fathers and mothers stayed together. Children were respectful and obedient.'

'I don't think life was ever totally like *Leave it to Beaver*.'

Haley knew she should stop, but couldn't. 'We used to be more — more cultured. Read Jane Austen novels, or watch the films they made from them. What beautiful, polite language they used, how nicely they dressed.'

'She wrote about the upper classes. There were far more people, I'm sure, who couldn't read or write at all, and spent their entire lives in dirty hovels trying to survive. Read Dickens.'

'Well, you may be right about that, but the middle class could be better, used to be better.'

He grinned. 'Okay, I give up. You do wish you lived in the past.'

'My grandmother often told me how they never locked their doors at night. No one scrawled graffiti on walls, and boys were taught to say 'Sir' and 'Ma'am' and help neighbor ladies with their bags of groceries.'

'But think of what you'd give up if you lived a hundred years ago: airplanes, television, indoor plumbing, microwave ovens — ' He paused. 'Velcro.'

Haley had to laugh, then sobered again. 'But I'd trade a few of those things for smarter people.'

'Don't you watch 'Jeopardy?' There are plenty of smart people around, even high school and college students. And many young people spend their summers helping to build houses for the homeless or visiting the elderly in nursing homes or working to save the environment.'

Haley knew about those things. Logic told her the cities weren't as bad as the local nightly news depicted them, but she seemed to have an emotional block and found it hard to accept. And because Jon was right, for a moment she didn't know how to answer. 'You're a very positive person, aren't you?'

'Call me a cockeyed optimist.'

She grinned, finished her tea and set

the cup down. 'I'm afraid I've been ranting. I'm sorry. Besides, I guess I ought not to detain you. You probably have things to do, bad guys to catch.'

'Not really. Since we're not having the excursion in Jacksonville, I have nothing to do. In fact, your losing your pin makes you the most important person on the train to me.'

'Do you plan to hover over me for the entire trip?'

'It's a thought. You're certainly the most attractive single woman on board.'

Once more Haley remembered his kiss and the way he'd held her in her cabin. But then she thought of the night before, when he'd tried to get chummy with the woman who came out of the shower, not knowing it was she.

'Be careful,' she said, 'you'll have me thinking you stole the pin yourself so you could spend more time with me.'

He snapped his fingers. 'Darn. I guess I wasn't smart enough to think of that.' He reached for her hand. 'But I'll gladly take advantage of it.'

Haley enjoyed the feel of his strong fingers on her palm but pulled away, once more remembering how he'd said similar nice things to someone else.

As if not noticing her gesture, he got to his feet. 'Actually there is something I must do, but have dinner with me again tonight. There's an interesting couple I want you to meet.' He glanced at his watch. 'Six-thirty?'

Haley felt ambivalent again. She was glad her comments hadn't turned him completely off, but she also knew she shouldn't spend so much time with him. If they continued this way, how would she ever say goodbye to him at the end of the trip?

But at least they wouldn't be alone for dinner that evening and she'd have a chance to get better acquainted with other passengers. She liked that.

Then she remembered something. 'Dinner on board? But weren't we supposed to do something in Jacksonville?'

'Because of our three-hour delay in starting, to say nothing of this rain storm, the excursion in Jacksonville has been cancelled.'

'Does everyone know about this?'

'Probably Walter Blaine announced it and we were too busy looking for your pin to notice.'

'Well, in that case . . . ' She grinned.

10

Haley pondered a long time over what to wear to dinner, not wanting to feel out of place. Except for the man who wore jeans to the reception — and whom she hadn't seen since — she'd noticed the passengers seemed to dress as if they were having dinner at the captain's table on a cruise. But the dress she'd worn the night before wouldn't do. Roberta had picked it out and the neckline was cut too low. She hoped the scarf she had pinned in place solved that problem, but she no longer had the pin anyway.

She pulled out a long plain black skirt over which she could wear a different blouse every time. That gave her a variety of looks without straining the capacity of her one suitcase. This time she chose the long-sleeved tunic with a paisley design in shades of silver and blue.

At precisely six-thirty she entered the dining car and Jon led her to a table for four. In a moment, an older couple joined them. Virginia Hofstetter was a middle-aged, slender woman who spoke with a Boston accent. Her husband Tom, who appeared to be a bit younger, had a round cherubic face under salt-and-pepper hair and a friendly outgoing manner.

Over the meal, Tom told them a fascinating story of how they had to smuggle their funds out of Germany at a time when there was a limit to how much money you could take out of the country.

'When the border guards searched the car, I knew we were headed for prison,' he said. 'I was sure they'd find the forty thousand dollars, our whole life's savings.'

'Where was it?' Haley asked.

'In the bottom of a tissue box on the back shelf of the car. They just kept shoving it from side to side, and never looked in it.'

After dinner, they left the dining car and Jon stopped in the vestibule between the cars, drawing Haley into his arms.

'Please,' she said, freeing herself, 'I think I'll just go to my cabin.'

'It's early,' Jon insisted. 'You can't go to bed yet.'

'But — ' She didn't know how to tell him what was on her mind. After all, she could hardly accuse him of flirting with another woman when she supposedly had no knowledge of it.

He steered Haley toward the observation car. 'Let's at least have some coffee.'

She let him lead the way and they sat on the round bench at the very rear. He turned to her and took her hand in his.

Once more she pulled her hand out of the well of his fingers and turned her head away from him, watching the steady rain pelt the windows. It blotted out the landscape, leaving only a fleeting impression of dark trees sliding noiselessly into the wake of the train.

His silence made her nervous. 'Do you think the rain will stop by morning?'

He didn't answer her question, but asked one of his own. 'What's the matter?'

'Nothing.' It came out in that clipped fashion of a small child who's been caught with his hand in the cookie jar.

'Don't give me that innocent stuff. I thought we had something — well, special, going on. Now, suddenly you're acting like I'm a leper.'

'I'm not — I mean — I like you very much and I think you're a very nice person, but . . . '

'But not for you, is that it?'

She looked into her lap, bit her lower lip. 'I'm sorry if you got the wrong impression.' She started to rise, but he clasped her hand tightly and she had no choice but to sit again.

He looked at her for a long time before speaking. 'I've been thinking about what you said earlier today. How you prefer the past to the present.'

128

Good, he was changing the subject. 'I'm sure I'm not the only person to feel that way.'

'But you sounded obsessive about it.'

Now that he mentioned it, Haley realized Roberta had often said the same thing. But so what?

'It made me think that something happened in your life to cause you to be that way. Something that made you afraid.'

'I'm not afraid. I just don't like — '

'I think you're afraid to fall in love.'

The very mention of love sent a shiver up her spine. How could preference for the past — or even fear — have anything to do with love? A flirtation on a train — which he seemed to want — was a huge way from falling in love. 'What makes you say that?'

'What hurt you? Tell me.'

'Nothing.' She pulled her hand from his. 'You're making a big leap if you try to connect my dislike of the present to fear of falling in love.'

He leaned closer, his voice low and

seductive. 'We're strangers on a train. You can tell me anything and it doesn't matter because we'll probably never see each other again.'

Haley turned away from his penetrating gaze. First he mentioned love, then he said they'd never see each other again, and that bothered her almost as much. But, her mixed-up emotions aside, the last thing she needed was to get involved with someone who would vanish from her life like petals from a dead flower.

'I think you've closed your mind to the possibility of love and marriage and all the stuff most women want. Why?'

'I'm not closed to it. I just don't think it will ever happen for me.'

'Why not? How old are you — thirty, thirty-two?'

She was surprised he came so close. Most men would have tried to flatter her by guessing mid- or late twenties.

'Thirty-five.' Why had she told him the truth? Of course, it didn't matter, because either their friendship would never escalate into anything more or it would, and he'd know the truth sooner or later anyway.

'I used to want those things,' she told him, 'but the right man just never came along and it's too late now.'

'It's not too late and you know it. I'll bet you've had dozens of men drooling over you. Why didn't you settle down long ago with one of them?'

Maybe they would drool over the blonde with the perfect make-up and fancy clothes, not her. 'I told you. They weren't right.'

'No, let me tell you. You're willing to start a relationship, but then, when it begins to look serious, you back off. You're afraid of something. Maybe it's my own background, but I can tell when people are afraid.'

'Don't be silly. I'm not afraid of anything. You may have been F.B.I., but you're not a psychiatrist.'

'Tell me about your background, your childhood. Do you have any brothers and sisters? Are your parents living? Were they happily married?'

She didn't answer.

'They weren't, were they? Something happened and now you distrust all men, even though you're not totally conscious of why.'

That time she managed to get up before he stopped her and she headed for the door. He was on his feet and behind her a moment later and followed her into the next car, saying, 'I'm sorry, but I hit a nerve didn't I? Why don't you talk to me about it? I'm a good listener.'

She ignored him and continued to her compartment. But when she tried to open the door, he held it closed, trapping her within the circle of his arms. She could feel her heart beating, or, since he was so close, was it his?

A passenger came down the corridor, tried to pass them to get to his own cabin, and, since there wasn't room for the three of them, Jon released his hold on the door, it pushed inward and he followed Haley inside. She dropped onto the couch, and Jon did the same, closer to the door.

'Talk to me, please,' he said.

Haley wanted very much to do that. She had felt comfortable with him from the moment they met, had enjoyed the feel of his arms around her, and had spent a good part of the day telling him how she felt about life. Her longing for a past that — as he had pointed out that afternoon — was probably never as rosy as she dreamed, was beginning to crumble. Only what she now recognized as her deep-seated resistance to getting involved with a man kept her from opening her mind and heart to the possibility of something good in the present. Roberta had been right and now Jon was telling her the same thing.

And he was not any man. He didn't get his feelings hurt, let his ego get in the way. She felt he genuinely wanted to know all about her, to understand what had kept her from marriage all those years. And he had already guessed the reason.

She took a deep breath. 'My father left home when I was six and my sister was twelve. My mother had to go to work to support us and we spent most of our days with our grandmother. It was like losing both a mother and a father. I guess you're right. I haven't really trusted men because of that.'

'And you work at a battered woman's shelter, where every woman you see has been abused by a man. No wonder you hate them.'

'I don't hate them.'

'But you don't want one of your own just in case he turns out to be like them.'

'Can you blame me?'

'No, but the odds against your having that kind of bad luck are sky high.'

'I told you, eleven hundred women came into our shelter last year.'

'Out of how many million who live in Denver?'

She knew instinctively that this was a small proportion, yet, emotionally she ached for every woman she saw with bruises and blackened eyes.

'Is your sister married?'

'Yes.'

'See? Is your friend Roberta married?'

'She was, but she's a widow now.'

'Was her marriage happy?'

'She says it was.'

'Do you have married friends? Are they happy?'

Haley thought of all the teachers at her school. Half had been divorced, but all but one had remarried and seemed to be making a go of it the second time.

He seemed to know her answer without her saying it. He leaned closer. 'Most people are good, most people are honest, most are trustworthy.' He paused. 'Do you have a credit card?'

'Yes, what's that got to do with — '

'If someone steals it and runs up bills are you obligated to pay them?'

'No, but — '

'Do you know why the credit card companies issue cards to people they don't even know, why they don't hold you liable for wrong charges? Because their losses from that sort of thing are less than one percent. Whenever I get discouraged — like watching the nightly news — I remember that and I tell myself, less than one percent of the people are dishonest. That means over ninety-nine percent are honest. Wow, what a great advantage.'

Haley couldn't help smiling. She'd never thought of those things before. Life had always seemed such a gamble. Her mother had had to work, and she had had to put herself through college. But she'd been able to get a partial scholarship. Now that she thought of it, some good person had given up some of his own hard-earned money so she could get an education. Suddenly she felt humble. She looked over at Jon. He believed what he was saying.

'I wish I could feel as you do.'

He got up. 'You can. Think about it. It's time you opened your heart to the possibility of making some guy happy.' He pulled her to her feet, put his arms around her and kissed her firmly.

The past, even the twenty-first century, seemed to disappear in a blaze of ecstasy. She felt she would melt from his touch, and wanted the moment never to end. But he released her, opened the door and left.

Weak and shaky, Haley fell onto the couch and sat still for a long time. In spite of all she'd said that night, she felt better than she had in a long time. The trip was wonderful and the people she'd met so far were good. And Jon? Besides being handsome and maybe the Prince Charming Roberta expected her to meet, he was the smartest and kindest person she had ever known.

But, if he was the genuine article, she was a fake, not the person he thought she was. She only pretended to be a *femme fatale* for a little while. He had already discovered more about her than anyone else ever had and it was only a matter of time before he'd also realize she'd been masquerading as a blonde.

There was only one thing to do about

it — keep their relationship on a just-friends basis. But after that kiss, could she possibly do that for five more days?

11

Once again Haley decided to shower at night before going to bed. She pulled off her wig and placed it in the expandable pouch, hung up her clothes and shrugged into the terry cloth robe. Then she realized her bed had not yet been made. What had kept Alan from doing it? Was he up to something? Jon had hinted that Alan — or one of the other porters — might be the thief he was looking for, but Haley couldn't believe Alan was his man. He probably had a perfectly legitimate reason for being a bit late.

Slippers on her feet, she opened her cabin door and peered out. The corridor was deserted. She listened for the sound of a vestibule door opening at either end of the car, but with the noise of the wheels over the tracks, as well as the fact that her cabin was virtually in the center, she heard nothing like that.

She walked swiftly down the corridor, having already learned that it was easier to keep her balance on the moving train by going faster rather than slower. However, she reached the shower door only to find it locked. Darn. She should have phoned ahead to make sure it was available. Apparently someone else had also decided that was a perfect time to use the room.

Now what? Should she go back to her compartment and make a reservation? She hadn't had to do that the night before. Or should she just wait for whoever was inside to leave? But if she waited and just followed the other person, it would not be clean. Perhaps there would be no towels for her use. She had towels in the lavatory in her own cabin, but that meant going back anyway, and if she did that, she might as well telephone.

Then the vestibule door opened and Jon came in. Damn the man. Was he always going to prowl through her car at that time of night? Once again, she was trapped. She couldn't go into the shower room and she couldn't go to her own cabin without him noticing which one she entered. She shrank back against the wall, hoping he'd just pass through to wherever he was headed.

'Hello,' he said, grinning at her. 'We meet again.'

Haley raised her voice an octave, as she had the night before when forced to talk to him without her blonde persona. 'Hello.'

'I feel I know you by now but you haven't told me your name.'

For some reason, she felt reckless. She'd been play-acting as a blonde with the wig, so now she'd pretend to be a different person without it. 'Caroline,' she said, making the last syllable rhyme with 'dine.' Appropriately, it was her grandmother's name.

'Well, Caroline, I keep hoping to see you during the day, but you must keep to yourself.'

Haley put on a southern accent, the only one she felt she could carry off convincingly. She'd heard a lot of southern accents in the past few days. 'You're right, Ah like to keep to mahself.'

Her dismissive words had no effect. If anything, he seemed more eager to get to know her. 'If we keep meeting like this, people will talk. Tell me when I can see you when you're uh — dressed.'

'Ah don't think y'all can.' Acting was one thing, but she needed to discourage him before he saw through her charade. 'Ah'm sorry, but Ah prefer to be alone.'

'A pretty girl like you should be having fun in the club car, meeting people, joining in the singing.'

'Thank y'all very much, but Ah'd rather not.'

He didn't give up easily. 'Perhaps some other time. This rainy weather has made everyone a little morose. When the sun comes out again, you may feel differently.'

'Perhaps. But now — '

'Of course, I'm keeping you from your shower. Good night, then.'

Haley put her hand on the knob of the shower door as if she'd pop in just as soon as he went on his way, and flattened herself as much as possible so he could squeeze by. As he did so, the edge of her robe attached itself to his trousers and the robe swung open, revealing a long expanse of bare leg.

He stared. 'Oh, my, yes, we shall have to see each other again.'

Haley snatched the robe closed and gave him an icy look, but he only grinned some more and took off in the direction of the other end of the car.

She no sooner decided the coast was clear, when the shower room door opened and Mrs. Draper stepped out, nodded to Haley and walked quickly down the corridor. Haley followed her, stepped into her own cabin and picked up the phone to make her shower reservation.

Twenty minutes later she was through with the shower and stood in the deserted corridor. Dried and clad in her robe, she made her way back and closed and locked her door, noticing with relief that her bed was made up by then.

She felt lucky that Jon hadn't recognized her, yet, at the same time, she was miffed that he flirted with her alter ego. She scolded herself for the feeling. Since she was only playing a part, why should she care if he looked for a substitute? In a way she wished she were the imaginary Caroline so he could romance her clone.

The train slowed down and finally stopped moving altogether. She raised her window shade a few inches and saw what appeared to be a railroad yard, with lots of other cars on sidings. She assumed they were in Savannah, Georgia, and guessed they were parked for the night. She wondered if she'd sleep as well with no motion to rock her.

★ ★ ★

Morning found the sun shining at last, and in the dining car people smiled and chatted, making an effort to get acquainted with their fellow passengers. The decibel level was considerably higher than it had been the day before. She was invited to join the honeymooners at their table and, after accepting the invitation, they exchanged pleasantries over breakfast.

The itinerary left on her bed the night before instructed passengers to be ready to leave the train at nine-thirty for their tour of Savannah, and everyone was to gather at the Seattle Club car. Those vestibule doors were open to the station platform and uniformed porters waited to help the passengers descend.

In spite of the sun and blue sky, Haley added her sweater to her outfit of light gray pants and matching shirt, then put the strap of her camera around her wrist and tucked her billfold, lipstick and cell phone into her handbag.

She boarded one of the two yellow

and red trolleys waiting in the station and after both were filled, with a total of about seventy people, a pretty girl wearing an Antebellum costume and a picture hat laden with flowers got on board. At the last moment, Jon also swung aboard and sat in a reserved seat behind the female driver. Haley watched him from her own seat and tried to quell her sudden accelerated heartbeat.

As the trolley started its journey into town, she couldn't pull her thoughts away from him and barely listened to the costumed tour guide, whose name was Leah. Using a hand mike, Leah — in a rich Southern drawl — told them about the sights they would see and the history of Savannah.

'Governor James Ogilthorpe founded the city in 1733,' she said, 'and he brought with him from England a lot of folks who had been in prison.' She waited while they absorbed that information, then added, 'Now, these were not your ordinary criminals: murderers, thieves, pickpockets and such like. Dear me, no. These were people who just happened to be poor and in debt. In those days, the British put folks in jail if they couldn't pay their bills — which, if you ask me, made it awfully hard for them to ever pay them — so Ogilthorpe decided to give them a fresh start in the new world.'

Leah paused and took a drink of water from the bottle resting next to her on the special front seat facing the trolley passengers.

'In exchange for his generosity in bringing them here,' Leah continued, 'he made three rules. There was to be no drinking of hard liquor — that was what had caused most of the men to be in debt in the first place. Second, they were to have no slaves. He wanted them to do all their own work, because work was good for them and they'd appreciate what they had much more if they did it themselves. And third, no lawyers were allowed to come, because lawyers just cause trouble.'

Haley joined in the laughter that

followed, although she suspected there might be a lawyer or two on that very trolley.

As they drove through the city, past the beautifully laid-out squares, Haley took advantage of the large window at her side to admire the views. Each square had a park in the center filled with azaleas and flowering trees, plus a church or public building, as well as stately homes, and whenever the trolley paused, Haley snapped pictures.

Eventually, they stopped for lunch, and Leah announced, 'This is the home of the coroner from John Behrens' book *Midnight in the Garden of Good and Evil*.'

As Haley stepped down from the trolley, Jon took her hand. 'It's just called, 'The Book,' here, and today our mint juleps are going to be served by the real Mandy, not Clint Eastwood's daughter who played her in the movie. Did you read the book or see the film?' he asked.

'Yes, both. I liked it.'

'I'll bet you do a lot of reading, as well as watching movies.' He looked at her as if thinking, 'instead of dating.'

Haley didn't have to respond because Leah made another announcement about lunch and everyone began moving toward the three-story white house.

Haley climbed the curving staircase up to the wide veranda that circled two sides of the house, leaving Jon behind to talk to some other passengers. She would have liked to have him all to herself, but knew he had to be polite to everyone.

While sipping her mint julep, she chatted for a moment with Mrs. Hofstetter and then followed the others inside where several long tables had been set up in the dining room, living room and entrance hall.

Lunch consisted of fried chicken and other delicious southern specialties and then they all piled into the trolleys again to go to another spacious and well-maintained mansion where several kinds of dessert were served. Once

149

more on board the trolley, Leah pointed out the houses where both Jim Williams and The Lady Chablis lived when Behrens wrote the book. The next stop was Fort Pulaski National Monument, but not everyone was required to go there. One trolley took those who wished to do so, and the other stayed in town so passengers could go shopping. Haley wanted to see the Fort, and not — she told herself — just because Jon was also going there. She planned to take notes of how the South had prepared for the Civil War, along with lots of snapshots. After all, the important purpose of the trip, she reminded herself, was to gain information for her students, not spend time with a man.

But this man had somehow managed to find a place in her heart and mind. For once in her life, she might finally fall in love. And yet, what about his attentions to Caroline the night before? Should that worry her? Yes, she knew Caroline didn't really exist, but he didn't. He had flirted with Caroline, not once, but twice.

A pain started in her middle, as if little daggers were in there trying to cut her new romantic feelings into a million pieces.

12

When the trolley disgorged the passengers, Haley walked all the way to the Fort, past the wooden buildings that once housed officers, and beside the long-abandoned soldiers' quarters. She climbed the narrow circular stairway leading to the top, where several cannons still pointed out into the distance.

Jon caught up to her there. 'If you lived a hundred and fifty years ago, you might have had a husband, father or brother fighting in the Civil War. I doubt you would have liked it very much.'

'I didn't say I wanted to live *that* long ago.' The sun warmed her and, as she walked on toward the cannons, she pulled off her sweater and tied the sleeves around her waist.

Jon followed close behind. 'About ninety years ago, we fought in World

War One. Seventy years ago, you'd have had a friend or lover fighting in World War Two, and been using ration stamps to buy meat and butter. After that came Korea, Vietnam and then Iraq.'

She had stopped at the far edge of the battlement and he came to her side. 'But things are somewhat better now. Today's bad grammar aside, for most people in the U.S. the present is not such a very bad time to be alive.'

She watched the slight breeze ruffle his hair and wondered what it would feel like to run her fingers through it. She forced herself to leave her musings and stick to the subject. 'I do hate war, so that's one for your side.'

'Here,' he said, reaching for her camera, 'let me take your picture so your students will know you were really here. Stand next to that cannon.'

She did as he asked, then saw him pull a small camera of his own out of his pocket and snap her again, which made her a little uncomfortable. Why did he want a picture of her?

She tried to ignore the puzzle and retrieved hers, taking two more snapshots of the area. Finally, looking down, she saw some of the other train passengers walking toward the exit. 'It must be time to get back on the trolley.'

As they approached the circular stairway leading down, Jon stepped in front of her. 'Here, let me go first so you won't fall.'

'See,' she said, as they slowly descended the worn, stone steps, 'gentlemen used to know such etiquette rules.'

'You mean that the man should go behind the lady going upstairs and in front of her downstairs?'

'Yes. No one does that anymore.'

He stopped and turned to her. 'I just did.'

She paused on the step just above him. 'You're an exception and I thank you for your thoughtfulness, kind sir.'

She waited but he made no move to continue down the stairs. Instead, since he was taller, his eyes were almost on a level with hers and he seemed to stare into them. She felt her heartbeat quicken again and was aware of how close they stood in the narrow stairwell, and of its musty odors. Out of the sunlight, she felt goosebumps rise on her bare arms. Yet in spite of the cooler air, her neck became damp with perspiration.

Jon reached out, pulled her against his chest, and kissed her lightly on the lips.

She backed away, but the step behind made her stumble and for a moment she was grateful he kept her from falling down. Nevertheless, she squirmed out of his arms. 'You shouldn't do that.' She sounded unconvincing even to her own ears.

'Sorry. It just seemed like the right time and place. We're all alone. You're very attractive — '

'Last night I thought we agreed to be no more than friends.'

'We did? I don't remember that. All I remember is having dinner with you, learning more about you, kissing you.'

She remembered all of that too, but, even with his arms around her, the old fears of starting something that could never become permanent returned.

'Let's just be friends,' she said. 'At least for now.'

He sighed, released her and continued down the stairs. 'Friends it is.'

They reboarded the trolley and Jon took his usual front seat while Haley took hers in the rear. She wondered if her face looked as flushed as it felt. Her mind focused on him, she couldn't stop thinking about his kiss on the stairs.

Eventually Leah's discourse penetrated her thoughts. She was discussing southern women of the period and the way in which they used their fans to indicate how they felt about a man. Southern women of the day were considered extremely delicate and often had the mysterious malaise, 'the vapors.' Jon added a few comments about what the men thought of all that. Soon they were trading jokes and the other passengers joined in.

Halfway back to town, the trolley

engine suddenly died, and the driver, a young woman named Kate, couldn't get it started again. Passengers began making suggestions about what to do, but Kate had a phone connection to headquarters and reported the problem was probably vapor lock. After advice from her boss on the other end, the driver tried to start the engine again and this time it caught. But not for long. It stalled again, and Leah said, 'It's got the vapors,' and everyone laughed again.

While another trolley was dispatched, Leah brought out a large thermos and began to pour Mimosas for everyone. Between the Mimosas and Leah and Kate's wise-cracking, no one seemed to mind the delay. Several passengers stepped down from the trolley and stood by the side of the road under a shade tree to wait. Haley got down and headed for a tree as well, and Jon caught up to her.

'May I refill your cup?'

'Yes, thank you. It's very refreshing.'

'We aim to please.' He reached for her empty cup and she felt a shiver trace up her arm when his fingers brushed hers.

'Of course, a hundred and fifty years ago, they didn't have disposable cups. Someone had to wash them by hand.'

'At least they weren't polluting the environment with plastic,' she answered.

He laughed. 'Okay, one for your side.'

When they transferred to the other trolley, and returned to the station and the train, Haley decided everyone seemed in a jolly mood and many passengers hugged Kate and Leah and gave them tips.

The merriment continued throughout dinner and singing around the piano in the club car that night. Haley joined in, feeling like a different person from the one who had boarded the train two days before. Her usual shyness around strangers, her reticence to initiate conversations seemed to melt away like snow in April. Part of her transformation, she was certain, came from the blonde wig making her feel like an entirely different person. But she also gave credit to Jon's pep talk the day before and the friendliness of everyone on the train. The camaraderie made her feel part of an exclusive club, membership in which was a privilege along with a responsibility to share and become a participant.

She felt confident that good things were happening and would continue. Her silver pin would be returned, too.

Jon came up to her at the piano while she and the Jacksons sang, 'Yes, Sir, That's My Baby.' When the next song began, he put his arm around her waist and leaned in to read the words on the sheet music that had been placed on the piano top, and she let him keep it there. It seemed the natural thing to do, and she told herself it was just a friendly gesture, not to be taken as a sexual overture. No matter how much she enjoyed it.

Very much later, as she prepared for bed, she rehearsed the day in her mind. Jon had been everywhere that day, helping where needed, filling in with information about Savannah and explaining all the activities. He had made sure the elderly lady with the cane was able to step up into the trolley and helped her down as well, to say nothing of making sure she could keep up with the others. He might really be on board only to find a possible thief, but he made an excellent activities director. Somehow she felt he would excel at anything he chose to do. Why did he leave the F.B.I, and that other job he had spoken of?

And then she remembered that brief kiss at the Fort. She brushed her fingers over her lips, still feeling the gentle pressure of his mouth. She was almost sad when she didn't run into him on the way to and from the shower room again. That time she might have flirted back.

13

Jon squelched the urge to wander through Istanbul car again in the hope of seeing Haley in the corridor. She might think they were only friends, but, in his opinion, their brief nocturnal encounters had elevated their relationship, adding both mystery and humor. He liked that.

But duty called. Although both Miguel the bartender, and Alan, Haley's sleeping car porter, remained on his list of possible suspects in the jewelry thefts, at the moment his concern centered on someone else who seemed suspicious. Not an employee this time, but a passenger. For a brief time, he'd wondered if Haley — because she unaccountably wore that wig — might be the thief, but — not only had she reported her own silver pin missing — he had come to know her well enough to realize she was incapable of such a thing. Or was his growing attraction to her getting in the way of his objectivity?

At this time, however, the person who attracted his attention was a man who was shown on the passenger list as Percival Vandeveer, but who resembled someone with such a name about as much as he did Napoleon. Percival — if that was his real name — was a big guy, over six feet, two hundred-plus pounds, mostly muscle, like he worked out seven days a week. He was young, mid-twenties maybe — born at a time when boys were named Jason, Brandon or Kyle, not Percival — wore casual clothes all the time, never took his breakfast or lunch in the dining car, and seemed to go out of his way to avoid people.

To be fair, that alone shouldn't make him suspicious. After all, unless he was a kleptomaniac, a person who could afford to buy a ticket on this train probably didn't need to steal things. In addition, there was no record of his being on the previous trip, the one in which jewelry went missing. No, the thing that had alerted Jon was the van.

When the trolleys returned to the train station that afternoon, Jon had noticed an old rusty-looking blue and white van — an ancient Volkswagon bus — in the parking lot. And, standing next to it, talking to two men wearing equally scruffy-looking clothes, was Percival Vandeveer. Or whoever he was. It didn't take a former F.B.I, agent to smell something rotten. He would just send a FAX to a certain person he knew and find out who Mr. Vandeveer was. If his suspicions were misguided, no harm would be done. But if his wild hunch was right, the man might be an imposter. And, perhaps, up to something nasty.

★   ★   ★

Although the train proceeded on its way to Charleston, South Carolina, during the late afternoon and evening, it stopped moving by bedtime and once again Haley fell asleep without the rocking motion. The next morning, seeing sunshine and a bright blue sky outside her window, she chose a short-sleeved blouse to wear with lightweight slacks. As she put them on, she suddenly realized that if she'd lived a hundred years before she'd be wearing high-necked dresses with long skirts over multiple petticoats, instead of comfortable pants. She wondered if Jon's ideas were beginning to get to her.

After breakfast she headed for the Seattle car vestibule to detrain and ran into Mrs. Draper in the corridor heading in the opposite direction. 'It's the other way,' she told her. 'We get off from the club car.'

'Oh, I'm not going,' Mrs. Draper said. 'I don't like all that walking. I'll just stay in my compartment and read my book.'

'Will you be all right alone?'

'Oh, I'm sure I won't be the only person staying on board. And there's always a porter stationed at the platform.'

Haley remembered that Mrs. Draper had been singled out during the reception on Saturday night as having ridden the train before, so she must know if not everyone took advantage of the side trips. Once again Haley supposed it was similar to what she knew of cruises: that some passengers stayed behind instead of going ashore at the ports of call.

She said, 'See you later then,' and continued to the exit. Although she thought it odd that a passenger didn't want to visit Charleston, she decided that perhaps the woman had been there before or else she just wasn't the sight-seeing type. Not everyone had the desire to learn about history as she did. In fact probably some people took that trip just for the glamour of the train and the gourmet meals. One of the teachers at her school, whose husband worked for an airline, flew to Boston once a year just to eat lobster.

Haley shrugged and hurried down the steps to join the other passengers and then boarded one of the two buses for their trip into town.

A Charleston tour guide, who was native to the area, boarded each bus, but Jon managed to board Haley's bus once more and, from time to time, added to the information the tour guide provided.

Her gaze stole to him constantly and she wondered if he'd find an opportunity to get her alone — as he had the day before when he kissed her at the fort. As they rode through the city, she focused her mind on the trip by taking copious notes about what she was learning and tried to forget her growing feelings for him.

She was surprised to find out that cotton was not the first and foremost crop of the South. That distinction belonged to rice. And slaves had been brought in from Sierra Leone in Africa because they were experts at growing rice.

'Because of rice, Charleston was the richest city in the South before the Civil War,' the guide said. 'And afterward it was the poorest. The owners couldn't afford to keep up their property, and homes fell into disrepair.'

Illustrating her remarks, the bus driver took them through sections of town where old — sometimes dilapidated — houses stood side by side with houses already restored, or being restored, to their former grandeur.

'In 1939,' the guide continued, 'the city council passed an ordinance that any building over seventy-five years old was considered a landmark and had to be preserved, so gradually, these wonderful old homes are being restored.'

Next, the buses drove through the countryside, then through large iron gates and onto the winding road of an immense former plantation, which the local historical preservation society was protecting. After going through the main plantation house, which had been preserved, although not restored, Haley strolled the grounds taking pictures, walking past ponds and streams, gardens with enormous banks of flowers, and stone statues.

Jon caught up with her, and her heart began that increased tempo she was beginning to associate with being in his company.

'Be careful where you walk,' he told her. 'Stay on the paths. They tell me that alligators often come up from the river.'

'Alligators? Are you sure?'

'The caretakers keep track of them and if they get too big they're taken away, but you could see some small ones, four or five feet.'

'Four or five feet? I don't call that small.' She looked around, but didn't see anything resembling an alligator at the moment.

'How are you enjoying the tour so far?'

'Very much. I'm learning things I didn't know before.'

'According to the old maps, slave

quarters used to be over there.' He pointed, and they walked over to a large rectangle of dirt edged in bricks, where a building had once stood. 'See,' he said, 'things are better than they used to be. We no longer keep slaves.'

Haley looked up at him. 'Aha, methinks I recognize another bit of your pep talk to make me happy I live now instead of a hundred years ago.'

'It couldn't hurt. In spite of the violence in so many movies and television shows, I think we have a greater reverence for life than we used to. In ancient Rome, for instance, chariots would simply run down anyone unlucky enough to be in the road at the same time.'

He took her arm and guided her over a small bridge, and once more she reacted to the feel of his hand on her bare arm.

'And, in the U.S.' he was saying, 'people leap into action when they hear of natural disasters. They send money, food and clothing to the victims of hurricanes, floods or earthquakes everywhere in the world.'

'But — '

'Alexis de Toqueville said it two hundred years ago: Americans are basically good.'

Haley wanted to retort that it might have been true two hundred years before, but not necessarily today. Yet, in all honesty, she had to admit that, so far as she knew, no call for help ever went un-heeded.

'Enough lecture for today,' Jon said. He looked at his watch. 'It's time to get back on board the bus and go to the next plantation. And lunch.'

'I'm glad to hear that. I'm starved.'

The next plantation, on the banks of the James River, had no standing mansion, only remains of a fireplace and a pile of bricks where it once stood. It had been destroyed, the guide had said, during the Civil War. Actually, what she said was that it had been destroyed by the 'Yankees,' but Haley hoped the old wounds had healed by then.

170

The grounds of the plantation were extensive, and sheep and goats wandered across a large expanse of grass between lanes that cut through the property. In one area, a large tent had been erected and tables and chairs set up for lunch. Haley took a seat at one of the round tables and soon young women in long cotton dresses covered in aprons, their hair swept up under cotton caps, served the lunch: salad and corn bread, followed by pecan pie and lemonade.

Afterward Haley wandered down by the river and sat on a bench under a tree. The combination of warm air and food had made her drowsy and she closed her eyes. Moments later, it seemed, Jon touched her arm.

'I think you'd better leave now or you could be lunch for that alligator.'

Haley leaped to her feet, turned and crashed into Jon's arms, only then daring to look at where she'd been sitting. A long gray-green alligator squatted less than ten feet away.

'You didn't tell me there were alligators here too. Would he really have attacked me?'

'I doubt it, but they didn't brief me on alligator habits. I was only told to keep guests from getting too close to the river.' He kept his arms around her. 'Do I get to claim I saved your life?'

As much as she enjoyed the feeling of being in his arms again, she grinned and pulled away, kept walking up the bank to higher ground. 'Yes, and I'll be eternally grateful. How's that for your ego?'

'Excellent.'

Haley noticed he had apparently left his blazer on the bus and the short sleeves of his white shirt showed off sturdy forearms. The taut fabric stretched over his well-muscled torso, his waistline was flat, hips trim. She began to imagine him without clothes, something that rarely entered her mind, and definitely not lately. She dragged her gaze away.

He reached for her camera. 'Let me

take a picture of you.'

Had he been thinking the same thing about her? 'I don't need a picture of me.'

'But you look so pretty with the sun shining on your hair.'

She winced and automatically touched the wig. She'd been wearing it so much during the past four days, she often forgot about it, but now she felt as fake as the blonde pageboy. To cover her discomfort, she gave him the camera. 'If that alligator is still around, try to get one of him. My thirteen-year-olds will love that.'

He retraced his steps down the bank, took a picture of the alligator and returned. 'Stay right there.'

She stood at the side of a flowering tree, with the river behind her, but then, just before she thought he was about to snap her picture, he stopped and handed the camera to one of the other train passengers who was walking by.

'Would you mind?' he asked.

The older man said, 'Not at all,' and in a second Jon hurried to Haley's side and the man took their picture, then returned the camera and walked off.

Haley continued to stand still for a moment, her mind focused on the thought that, when she looked at the pictures, she'd remember Jon. But then, she'd always remember him, wouldn't she? She took the camera from his hand and they walked in silence for a few minutes. Was he thinking what she was thinking? Would he remember her long after today? If he did, he'd visualize that blonde woman, not the real Haley. But there was nothing she could do about that.

A wooden building came into view. 'Are you going to hit the gift shop before we get back on the bus?' he asked.

Haley came out of her reverie. 'I really think I should. If I find something unique, I can do 'show and tell' for my classes.'

'You're an exceptional teacher.'

She flushed at his praise. 'Not really. And whatever money I spend will go for a good cause. I'm grateful that historical societies keep places like this available to the public.'

'Some try, but I admit we could do better in this country. Europe is filled with beautiful buildings that have been around for hundreds of years, but here, too often, we tear them down to build something modern.'

'Or glamorous, like a gas station or parking lot.'

Jon laughed. 'Touche'.'

'One for my side?' she asked.

'Don't worry, I'll think of several things to offset that by tonight.'

'Tonight?'

'At dinner. You *are* having dinner with me again, aren't you? I want you to meet the Ellisons from California.'

'Is that part of your job as activities director, to spend plenty of time with passengers, introduce them to one another, and make them feel special?'

'Do you feel special?'

'Of course.' She tried to sound flip about it, but 'special' seemed an inadequate description of her mood whenever she was with him. She hurried on. 'Or is this part of your secret agent job, trying to figure out who might be a thief? How's your investigation into my missing pin coming, anyway?'

'Unless the office returned it to you, I'd say there was nothing new on that front.'

'Has anyone else reported jewelry missing?'

'No. And I hope it stays that way.'

'So do I. You said a member of the crew is more likely to be guilty and I keep watching Alan when he comes to my cabin, but so far at least, he hasn't done anything suspicious. Of course,' she added, 'I don't think I'd know what's suspicious anyway. Yesterday, before we got back on the train, I saw him in the station talking to someone, but that's all.'

'Talking to what kind of someone? A man or a woman?'

'A man.'

'Can you describe him?'

Haley stared at him, suddenly feeling tense and uncomfortable. 'You think it's important, don't you? But why?'

'Alan is from New York, never been out of that city, he says, until now. I have to wonder how he could know anyone in Savannah.'

'It could have been a relative. Families do split up, you know. Or just someone who noticed his uniform and asked him questions about the train.'

'You're right, of course, but, on the other hand, if he stole your pin — or anything else — he might pass it on to someone else to sell for him.'

'That seems rather far-fetched to me.'

'Maybe so, but, when an investigation is going on, nothing should be overlooked.'

'Okay, Sherlock Holmes, the man he spoke to was medium height, medium build, had medium-length brown hair, wore sunglasses and dark clothes.' She paused. 'Just like a million other men in the world.'

Jon smiled at her. 'You're quite observant, aren't you? You're right, that description fits a lot of people, but I'm glad to have it anyway. And, from now on, I'll watch Alan's movements more closely.'

'Since he's the porter in my car, I thought he was your prime suspect.'

'Not really.'

'Who then?'

'I'd rather not say. I could be wrong.'

'Some other employee, like a bartender or waiter?'

'I can t say.'

Haley shrugged and dropped the subject, but she was sure Jon suspected someone else who worked on the train. She'd found everyone to be unfailingly polite and helpful — with only seventy-five passengers and a crew of forty, pampering went without saying — but she supposed it was possible for a snake to live in this particular Eden.

She just hoped that stealing was all

this one had on his mind, and she was grateful she could at least lock her cabin door when she was inside. In spite of the heat of the day, she shivered. She'd been only joking when she told Roberta she might end up a blonde corpse.

14

Jon stopped at Haley's door and suggested they have a drink in the club car before dinner, and while she changed clothes, he went to the office to check on his inquiry of the night before. A FAX had come in for him, revealing — among other things — that Mr. Percival Vandeveer was a resident of New York, widowed and seventy-two years old.

The hairs rose on the back of his neck. Where was the real Vandeveer and why was someone on board pretending to be him? Possible explanations ricocheted through his mind. First, Mr. Vandeveer could have died between signing up for the trip and the actual date of departure and someone else decided to use his ticket. Unlikely, since the FAX revealed the man had been alive on Saturday. Second, he could have decided not to take the trip after all and given the reservation to a friend or family member. But, again, the thought that the man on board could be even remotely acquainted with Vandeveer, who was worth a cool ten million dollars, beggared the imagination.

But the main reason why Jon remained suspicious was, again, the van. When they returned from Charleston, the same blue van sat at the far end of the parking lot. Jon could not mistake the aging Volkswagon, its formerly white top peppered with rust, even if he hadn't recognized the Florida license plate. Why would such a van be chasing the train up from the South unless there was some skullduggery involved?

But what? It was too early to question the man taking Percy's place, in case there was some totally innocent explanation. False accusations could result in hefty lawsuits. He'd like to talk to him in an informal atmosphere, but until that happened, there were other things he could do. He prepared and sent off another FAX.

★　★　★

Haley exchanged her casual pants outfit for the same long black skirt she'd worn the night before, this time pulling a scoop-necked raspberry-colored silk tunic over it, and met Jon in the club car.

Seated next to him with a glass of wine, she once more brought up the subject of his background. Even though she might never see him again after the trip, she felt as if she needed to know everything about him. 'Did you always live in Portland?'

'Yep. My great-grandparents crossed the country on the Oregon trail and settled there.'

'Went to school there and everything?'

'Willamette University in Salem, just like everyone else in my family.'

'But you don't live in Oregon now.'

'I did graduate work at Cornell. Then my dad wanted me to work for him, but I thought that was too dull. Instead, I headed for Washington and wangled my way into the F.B.I.'

'Were you with the F.B.I, *before* or *after* that corporation you worked for?'

'Which corporation?'

'The one with the back-stabbers you didn't like.'

'Oh, that one. Before.' He paused and sipped his wine. 'But my wife didn't like the idea of my being gone a lot on jobs I couldn't talk about, so I quit. Kind of a shame after all that training.'

'But that was very considerate of you.'

'Turns out I needn't have bothered. I took a nine-to-five job but we broke up anyway.' He paused again, ran a hand through his hair. 'Look, I don't mean to make her out as the bad guy. We just didn't see eye-to-eye on some basic things. That's a problem when you marry young. You may change your mind about what you want out of life.'

Haley decided it had been his wife's change of heart that broke up the marriage. 'What did she want out of life that you didn't?'

'It's what she didn't want — children.'

He glanced at his watch, and Haley took that as a signal he didn't want to discuss the topic of his former marriage any more.

'You said you play racquetball sometimes. Any other hobbies?'

'I coached middle-school kids in basketball and baseball for awhile. I'd like to do that again.'

Haley figured that had been the outlet for his nurturing side. She wished he'd come to her school. They needed coaches.

'And I cook a little.'

'You cook?'

'Well, living alone so much, it became a necessity. Eating in restaurants all the time gets old in a hurry.'

'And expensive,' Haley added.

He paused before answering. 'That too. And I love to travel.' He grinned, set his glass down and took her hand to pull her to her feet.

'And now I think we'd better combine travel and eating and go to the dining car. We don't want to keep the Ellisons waiting.'

The Ellisons were an elderly couple who had been everywhere. They had ridden the Orient Express from Paris to Istanbul, visited every country in Europe and Asia, had cruised on the Queen Elizabeth II, flown the Concorde, sailed up the Nile in Egypt, visited giant tortoises in the Galapagos and penguins in Antarctica.

'You must really love to travel,' Haley said.

'We have no children,' Ellison explained, running a hand through his sparse white hair, 'and all our other family members are gone now.'

Mrs. Ellison touched her husband's arm in a loving gesture. 'We only travel half the year. The rest of the time we manage a foundation that provides scholarships for disadvantaged children.'

'That sounds like a lovely thing to do.'

'The highlight of our year is seeing some of those children graduate from a university.'

In spite of their obvious financial independence, and the good work they were doing, Haley felt sorry for their having no children of their own and thought again about her desire to have a child while still possible.

'With all that foreign travel, I would imagine you've already been everywhere in the United States too.'

'We did travel across the country rather extensively many years ago, but things change and it's fun to go back.'

'Do you have a favorite destination or mode of travel?' Haley asked.

'I like this train,' Ellison said. 'We have a large bedroom that's quite comfortable, with our own shower, and it's so much easier than enormous airports and airplane travel.'

'You don't find the train too confining?' Jon asked.

'Hardly. Confining is on an airplane when the person in front of you puts his seat back down in your face.'

'I'm a bit claustrophobic,' Mrs. Ellison said, 'and when they do that, I feel as if I'm in a coffin. Thank goodness we can afford to fly first class, where the rows are a bit wider apart. Even so, I always take a book along — preferably a mystery — because it keeps me from thinking about feeling closed in.'

She fingered a pearl choker at her neck, and Haley wondered if it was very valuable and if she should warn her there might be a thief on board. But Jon was sitting right there next to her. He should be the person to remind her to put valuables in the office safe. She turned to him, but, if such a thought crossed his mind, his face gave no hint.

'But you get places so much faster on a plane,' Jon was saying.

'Don't get us wrong,' Ellison said, 'we like plane travel too, but traveling like this is, well, like reliving our youth when trains were the only civilized way to go.'

Haley wanted to tell Jon that was exactly how she felt, but instead she just glanced over at him with a knowing smile. He reached for her left hand in her lap and gave it a squeeze, as if to say he understood her thoughts.

'I'm glad you like our facilities,' he said. 'The company spent fifteen million dollars restoring these cars to their original beauty.'

'It certainly shows,' Mrs. Ellison said. 'We're going to go west on the train later in the year, through Utah and the Rockies.'

They lingered over dessert and coffee, Haley listening avidly to their descriptions of places she'd never seen and the history behind them, wishing she had her notebook with her.

Ellison described seeing the Passion Play in Oberammergau, Germany, in the year 2000. 'They only do it once every ten years, you know,' he said. 'But they began doing it because of the plague.'

'The Black Death in Europe in the fourteenth century?' Haley knew the story but could see Ellison was eager to tell it, so she didn't make any further comment.

'Yes, the town of Oberammergau was spared for a long time because they didn't let people in or out. But then one young man came to see his sweetheart — '

'Ah, love is stronger than borders,' Jon said, glancing at Haley.

' — and he brought the disease with him. Three people died and then the town fathers held a meeting and prayed. They promised God that if the plague would go away, they would put on a Passion Play once every ten years for all eternity.'

'I guess it worked,' Jon said.

'You should go there,' Mrs. Ellison said. She looked questioningly first at

Haley and then at Jon, as if assuming they were a couple.

Jon turned to Haley. 'Let's do that, shall we? Remind me in 2009 to make reservations for the next one.'

Haley gave him a stern look, but didn't answer. Her heart had started thumping at the look he had given her earlier besides the thought they'd be together in the future. Finally, she put her napkin on the table next to her empty coffee cup. 'I think the waiters would like to clear the table. Almost everyone else has already gone.'

'We'll say good night, then,' Ellison said. 'It was a pleasure to dine with you this evening.'

The Ellisons wove their way through the dining car, and Jon steered Haley to the club car.

'Let's listen to Gaynor play some more, shall we?'

The long walks in Charleston had apparently worn out some of the passengers and there were not as many as usual in the car or around the piano.

Gaynor was playing a slow, romantic song and Jon moved a coffee table out of the way, took Haley in his arms and they began to dance.

He sang softly in her ear, his voice not a bit like a rusty hinge, but well-modulated. 'You must remember this, a kiss is still a kiss — '

She remembered his kiss only too well. Although she wanted to feel his lips on hers again, considering the trip would come to an end in three more days, she doubted she ought to encourage more of the same. She looked up at him. 'You let the Ellisons think we were — well, together.'

'We are together.'

'But they meant — well, you know what they meant, and I won't be seeing you in 2009 to remind you to make reservations for the Passion Play.'

'But we could go together, couldn't we? We could make a date for spring of 2010 and no matter where we are or what we're doing, we'll meet at JFK airport and fly to Germany to see the

Passion Play together.'

'You sound like that film, *An Affair to Remember* where they promised to meet in six months' time on top of the Empire State Building.'

'Well, we *could* make it the Empire State building if you'd rather.'

That had been another Cary Grant movie, and he and Deborah Kerr — a redhead that time, not a blonde — met on a cruise ship and fell in love. And here she was on a train — but it was like a cruise ship on land — and he wanted to meet her again. Her throat choked up and she couldn't answer.

Gaynor swung into the next song without a break, and Haley settled into Jon's arms, their cheeks touching, and he hummed the melody while Gaynor sang, 'For all we know, we may never meet again — '

Jon's hinting that they'd see each other again after the trip was slowly banishing her doubts. She thought of all those years of negative thinking that were yielding to his optimism, charm and intelligence. She relished that moment with him and any others they were likely to have. He danced beautifully, held her so close she could smell the clean scent of his skin, feel the strength in his arms and thighs. For a little while longer, she'd pretend she was not Haley Parsons, the mousy schoolteacher, but a blonde adventuress who danced with handsome men, made them fall in love with her and then left them waiting on top of the Empire State Building with broken hearts.

Song followed song without a pause, as if Gaynor knew they wanted her to go on all night long, never stopping.

But she did stop and Haley realized it was after eleven. She pulled away from Jon, who seemed not to want to let her go, and said, 'I think we've closed up another car. Even the bartender has disappeared.'

'I'll walk you home,' Jon said.

As they maneuvered their way through the vestibule between the Berlin and Istanbul cars, he stepped to the side and pulled her with him.

She raised her voice over the noise of the train wheels. 'Why are we stopping?'

'Look out there. See the moon?'

She edged closer to the door, where someone had left the window down, and looked out at a perfectly full moon against the black sky. The wind pulled at her hair, the cold night air stinging her cheeks, and she backed up. Jon stood behind her, leaning against the car wall, and he put both arms around her waist, hugging her to him. She felt the warmth of his body at her back, the strong muscles in his thighs against her legs, and a sudden rush of desire clutched her. In spite of the cold and the noise, she didn't want the moment to end.

'There's a city out there,' he said, his mouth and warm breath at her ear. 'See the lights?' He pulled one arm free to point again, and as he did so, he brushed against her breast, setting off sparks in her body and brain. She hoped he'd do it again and he did when he replaced his arm around her waist, this time higher on her midriff. Her legs trembled.

He nestled his head in the crook of her neck, kissed her bare shoulder where her blouse had pulled to one side. She turned her head, knowing he would kiss her mouth if she did. Wanting it.

The door of Berlin car opened and a middle-aged, plump man came through. Haley felt herself stiffen, waiting for the man to go on through the vestibule. But he didn't. He stopped and lit a cigarette, then, finally noticing Haley and Jon in the corner, crossed between the cars to take his smoking break on the other side. But it was too late. He was still too close, and the mood was broken.

Jon pulled his arms from around her waist and took her hand to cross into Istanbul car. He opened the heavy door and they went through, then walked slowly to 'E' cabin. At her door, he pulled her to him and kissed her. He kissed as expertly as he danced, his lips firm and warm, pressing just the right amount. She felt her knees buckle.

He held her tightly with one arm and opened her door with the other hand. He came inside and closed the door behind them. Sweeping aside the mint on the pillow and the next day's itinerary, he pulled her onto the already made-up bed.

He kissed her again and this time her arms went around him and she arched her body into his. She had never wanted a man as she did this one.

Still kissing her, he lowered her head onto the pillow and his hands explored her curves, pressed her hips. She couldn't breathe. Her face felt flushed, her hair on fire.

Her hair! Suddenly she remembered that was not her real hair fanning out across the pillow, but a wig. If this love-making — and it was love-making, wasn't it? — went on much longer, her wig would come off. It already felt as if it was slipping out of place — and then where would she be? Exposed for a phony.

She managed to turn her head away from his lips, put one hand on her head to keep the wig in place, and inched off the bed. 'Sorry,' she said. 'I'm afraid I got carried away.' She stood against the sink, gasping for breath.

'Beautifully carried away,' he said, rising to stand next to her. He started to put his arms around her. 'And you weren't the only one.'

'We mustn't do that,' Haley said in a voice that sounded strange and hoarse. 'We settled this question, remember? I'm not — '

'It's a lady's prerogative to change her mind, and I'm pretty sure you changed your mind about me sometime tonight.'

She took a few deep breaths. 'Too much wine.'

'You only had one glass at dinner, hours ago.'

' — the music — '

'Lovely music, music we'll always remember.'

Yes, she would never hear those

songs again without thinking of him. 'You'd better go.' She managed to reach for the door handle and pull the door open. Doing so made her back up farther, pressing her even more firmly into his arms.

'Are you sure?' he whispered in her ear.

'Yes,' she whispered back, keeping her face turned away lest he kiss her again and she'd throw sanity to the winds.

After a long moment in which she thought time had been repealed, he dropped his arms and maneuvered past her to the door. He stepped into the corridor and looked back at her. 'Until tomorrow.'

She closed the door, and turned the lock before she could change her mind and invite him back in. Her heart gave a short, sharp pull. Her body ached to have him close again, and longings she hadn't felt in years swept over her. She knew she wanted this love affair, but it seemed impossible. She couldn't make love to him without revealing her real self. And then, what if her deception all that time made him angry? What if, when he learned the truth, he'd never want anything to do with her again?

15

After several minutes, and a glass of water, Haley calmed down enough to start her normal bedtime routine. She pulled off the wig and, since the expandable pouch under the window was already filled with itineraries and postcards, stuffed the wig into the pouch in the lavatory. She removed her clothes, pulled on the terry cloth robe, and headed for the shower. Bathed, dry and wrapped in the robe again, she opened the shower door only to slam it into someone in the corridor. Who else but Jon?

A cry of frustration caught in her throat.

He took hold of her hand and pulled her into the corridor. 'Caroline?' he said brightly. 'What a treat to see you again.'

To keep him from realizing she was Haley, not Caroline, she averted her face from the dim light of the small hallway fixture.

His hands on her elbows, he seemed determined to keep her close, so she tilted her head down into the collar as far as she could, found herself staring at the belt of her robe, which — she saw with dismay — was not tied tightly. It might come loose with the slightest wrong move. She remembered that the last time she'd encountered Jon like that, one end of the robe had attached itself to his trousers and had fallen open.

'I've missed you,' Jon said. 'I didn't see you last night and I worried. I've become very fond of our midnight rendezvous.'

Haley's body tensed and her face grew hot. How dare he? Just moments ago he had been ready to make love to her and now he was coming on to *her*. She had a sudden flash of the film *On a Clear Day You Can See Forever* and Yves Montand falling in love with the eighteenth century character he had found by hypnotizing the twentieth century Barbra Streisand. Why, for heaven's sake, did everything about this trip remind her of a movie? Had her life been so drab for the past fifteen years that her only thoughts came from make-believe people and plots?

But the man holding her arms was real. Jon was not Cary Grant or any other admirable film character. He was just another man who would betray a woman if it pleased him. She wanted to kick him in the shins, but her slippers were too soft. She wanted to punch him in the nose, but he still held her arms. Most of all, she wanted to curse him for the two-timing rat he was, but to do that she would have to reveal she'd been passing herself off as a blonde. She wasn't brave enough to do that. She would continue the charade tonight, but he would never find Haley in his arms again. Let him romance Caroline! If he could.

She put on her high Southern voice. 'Let me go please.' She added, 'You're hurting me,' although he really wasn't. But it made him drop his hold and she squeezed past him and ran down the corridor.

What now? She couldn't go into her cabin or he would see. She kept going, into the next sleeping car, and tried the door of that shower room. It opened and she ducked inside before he had even followed her to the end of the Istanbul car. She hoped he would have no idea where she'd gone.

She locked the door and sank down on the wooden bench, praying that no one wanted to use the room, and that Jon would give up and go away. Why was he always in her car at night anyway? Sure, he was supposed to be looking for a possible thief and thought that Alan, her car porter, might be the one, but what did he hope to learn at this time of night, when all the passengers were in their cabins, sleeping, with their doors locked?

She was too tired and too angry to puzzle it out. After her breathing returned to normal, she opened the door and gingerly headed back to her own compartment. That time, thank goodness, the corridor was completely empty.

She slipped out of the robe, put on her night-gown and crawled into bed, but the memory of Jon being there with her earlier kept her awake. Why did he have to behave that way? When she was herself, the nondescript school-teacher, men might double-cross her, but that wasn't supposed to happen to the blonde she had become for the train trip. And she had liked him so much. She had spent hours with him, enjoying his intelligence and humor, learning to see the world a little differently because of his optimism, feeling like a desirable woman. How could he be a sweet, charming, helpful person one moment, and deceive her the next? Tears welled up in her eyes and slid down her cheeks. She buried her face in the pillow and sobbed until she fell asleep.

★　★　★

The train moved all the next day, heading for Richmond, Virginia. Haley — recovered from her humiliation of the night before and determined not to let him hurt her again — vowed to avoid Jon. She went to the observation car for breakfast only to discover her stomach was still tied in knots and she could force down very little. She skipped lunch altogether. That should have enabled her to elude Jon, but he managed to find her anyway, and she could only retreat to her compartment, lock herself in and tell him to go away.

'I never want to see you again,' she said through the door.

'What's the matter? What have I done?'

She couldn't tell him the truth and was afraid even to start a conversation. She wouldn't answer. Finally he went away, either because he felt foolish talking to a closed door or because he had work to do.

The train pulled into Richmond at three that afternoon and backed into a siding near the old station. According to the itinerary, a new, modern station had been built and the old building turned into a science museum and IMAX theater. Passengers were free to walk over to that building, and Haley decided that a good documentary might take her mind off her current unpleasant thoughts

Since it had begun to rain, she put on her raincoat and tied a scarf over her wig before stepping down from the train. A young woman employee stood ready to assist everyone and Haley felt sorry for her.

'How awful to have to stay outside in this rotten weather.'

'Oh, it's not so bad,' the girl admitted. 'We take turns at the door.'

'You mean someone has to be here all the time?'

'Oh, yes. We can't let any unauthorized people board the train. That's why all the passengers have badges, you know.'

'But mine is covered up by my coat.'

'Oh, I recognize you. If I didn't recognize someone, I'd just ask to see their badge.'

Head down against the blustery wind and water, Haley hurried toward the science museum, wondering if that particular security measure was always in place or if Jon had instigated it.

Jon. She'd have to stop thinking about him. Inside the science museum, she returned her thoughts to her students. How they would enjoy that. Several large rooms contained exhibits and hands-on experiments that illustrated scientific principles or physics problems. She watched a pendulum, looked at optical illusions, and even took a make-believe taxi ride where the driver — on a video screen — discussed how to drive safely.

Next she sat in front of a mirror that showed what her face would look like if the right half were exactly the same as the left half. Then, she could change the image and see how she looked with two left sides. Amazingly, she looked quite different. Almost like the difference between herself with the blonde wig and without.

She left the museum in time to see the IMAX movie, which was a documentary about building the Three Gorges Dam across the Yangtze River in China. Still under construction at the time of the filming, the dam, the narrator pointed out, would cost twenty billion dollars but was expected to save that much every year when the river no longer flooded, killing people and ruining lands downstream. But the Yangtze is a huge river and the dam would be over a mile across and six hundred feet high, so large it would be visible from space.

Surrounded by the huge screen, Haley felt as if she were right there on the construction site, inside the cabin with the female crane operator who moved huge blocks of stone, or walking a bridge that would soon no longer be above water. The narrator told how many thousands of people were being moved to higher ground, how many villages — some of them four thousand years old — would disappear forever. Worst of all, ancient temples, and even an excavation site where antiquities were being discovered, would end up a hundred feet under water.

To Haley's dismay, the lake would actually be on top of an earthquake fault, and some anti-dam groups were predicting disaster. That was countered by experts who insisted every possible contingency had been taken into consideration.

But Haley felt compassion for all the Chinese people having to leave their homes, construct new villages and learn how to grow food in what amounted to a different climate at a much higher elevation. Once more she felt that new things were not always better. Would those people really prefer the electricity and possible safety the dam provided, or would they rather live the old ways? She was pretty sure that if she lived there, she'd be anti-dam, but probably Jon would say she was just anti-progress.

Jon. The infuriating man was always popping up in her thoughts, in spite of her resolve to keep him out. She pushed his vision aside and, when the film ended, she left the theater and hurried back through the continuing downpour to the train. That time a young man stood outside the one open door, but, he, too, seemed to recognize her and didn't ask to see her badge.

Before hanging up her raincoat, she removed her billfold and cell phone from the pockets and put them into the expandable pouch in the lavatory, then put on the new red dress Roberta had insisted she buy, a long skirt with a long-sleeved tunic. The fabric was heavier than her other clothes, just right for the cooler weather farther north, and the top was plain so the necklace Roberta had lent her came out of its velvet box and she placed it around her neck.

The necklace was very old — even old-fashioned — consisting of intricate gold chains woven together and, hanging at the base, an ornate design of gold filigree with precious gems: tiny sapphires, rubies and yellow diamonds. The pendant hung just above her breasts and completed the luxurious effect. She wondered what Jon would think of her appearance. She visualized herself standing before him in the beautiful red dress, imagined his brilliant smile, the admiration glowing in his eyes. Oh, why had he turned out to be a two-timer?

Jon. She'd have to find a way to escape having dinner with him, and when she entered the dining room, she saw an opportunity. Mrs. Wolski, the woman with the cane, whom Jon had so often aided, sat alone at a table for two.

'May I join you?' Haley asked.

'Yes, please.' Mrs. Wolski smiled, her pale blue eyes lighting up. In her seventies, Haley imagined, the woman had a few wrinkles around her mouth and eyes, and pure white hair, which was pinned into a neat, twisted coil at the back of her head.

Haley sat down saying, 'I'm Haley Parsons.'

Mrs. Wolski reached one blue-veined hand across to her. 'I would very much like you to company me.'

Haley hadn't realized the woman had an accent, but Mrs. Wolski soon explained. 'I don't speak the English too good. When we came to this country from Poland, I learned, but my husband, he worked and I stayed at home with the children. Now I'm alone, so I try to practice English more.'

'I think you speak it quite well,' Haley said.

They ordered their meal and she asked if Mrs. Wolski was enjoying the train trip.

'Yes. My son is give me this vacation. He is very smart boy, makes lots money. Only in America could he do so well. We are very grateful to be here.'

'What does your son do?'

'He started business — make something for automobiles — and now he is head of big corporation. He has wife and three children. My grandchildren,' she added. 'You are married? You have children?' she asked Haley, then answered her own question. 'No, I think you are not married. You are alone, no?'

'Yes, I'm alone. I've never been married and have no children.'

'That is too bad. You should marry, have a son like mine who takes good care of you in old age.'

Haley didn't answer because their soup arrived and they ate in silence. But when they were served salad and rolls, Mrs. Wolski took up the topic again.

'You are not married but you have admirers, yes? That nice young man, Mr. Shafer, he looks at you all the time. Is something — ?'

Haley felt her cheeks flush. 'No, nothing. We're just — friends.' At the moment, enemies seemed nearer the truth.

'Friends is good. From friends comes love. I know. My husband and I were good friends first. That kind lasts, not the other.'

Haley changed the subject to the

weather, then asked where Mrs. Wolski lived.

'In Maryland, in very lovely home. It is — what do they call it — retirement home.'

'Your son doesn't have you live with him?'

'No. I like better this way. He has family, they need privacy. But he visits often and I spend holidays in his house.'

With the entrees, Haley asked Mrs. Wolski if she had flown to New Orleans to get on the train.

'No, I start the trip in Washington, go to New Orleans and then come back same way.' She grinned as if it was a superior way to travel.

'But, it's the same trip, just in a different direction. The same stops and the same sights.'

'Yes, I don't mind. I see some of them one direction, some in other. That way I don't have to get off every time if I don't want to.'

Haley was thinking it cost twice as much, but didn't say it aloud. Mrs.

Wolski, however, apparently read her mind.

'My son pays for this. He is good to me.' She paused. 'Also, this way, he takes me to the train and picks me up again when I come back.'

'Then Mrs. Draper is not the only person on the train who's done this before. At the reception the first night they pointed out that she was traveling with them again. But they didn't mention your name.'

'My son pay for ticket. Maybe they put his name instead of mine for trip back.' She paused, frowning. 'I remember Mrs. Draper from other time.'

Haley thought she detected a hint of scorn, as if Mrs. Wolski didn't like the other woman. She'd have thought that, since each was traveling alone, they might have become friendly. But what did she know?

'I'm so happy for you,' Haley said. 'You really do have a wonderful son.'

'He pays for retirement home too. Is very nice. My own apartment with my own things. I like being with people there. They have same memories like I do. We talk about old times. We play canasta and mah jhong too.'

Haley visualized the woman in her retirement home, living life the way she preferred with her own friends and interests. Some day, she, too, might live in a retirement home, but she had no wealthy son who might pay for it. Or any son at all.

Mrs. Wolski seemed to read her mind again. 'You must marry, have sons too, like mine.' She paused. 'I think Mr. Shafer would like same thing.'

'Mr. Shafer and I — ' She stopped. She couldn't explain the whole, strange mess.

'I think you have quarrel, and that is why you don't sit with him tonight. Don't be too quick, my friend. Make up with him. Then you be happy, smiling again, like before.'

Once more Haley changed the subject. 'Will you be taking any other train trips?'

'I think yes, but I must convince doctor first.'

'You look healthy. Why doesn't the doctor want you to travel any more?'

'He says my heart is bad. Too much excitement, strain, is bad for me.'

'But he let you come this time.'

'I had to argue.' She chuckled, as if remembering the argument.

'What did you say?'

Mrs. Wolski sat up straighter in her chair, dramatizing it. 'I say to him, 'For what are you save me? I am going to die one day. Why just sit and wait? Maybe next year I need a walker instead of cane. Maybe wheelchair. Then I can't get on train.''

Haley sympathized. She knew the narrow corridors in those old railroad cars couldn't accommodate walkers or wheelchairs.

'So I say to him, 'If I die on train now then I don't die in my bed later. I save you the trouble.''

Haley laughed at that. She really liked the woman, even if she did seem to want to throw her and Jon together.

Jon. She looked around and finally saw him sitting at a table with the Jacksons. Perhaps he had just ordered, and wouldn't be finished for some time. With luck, she wouldn't have to meet him at all that night. Mrs. Wolski had been fortunate to marry her friend and live happily ever after, but real life wasn't always like that and the woman didn't really know Jon at all.

Their meal finished, Haley thanked Mrs. Wolski for her company and headed back to her cabin. She wouldn't go to the club car that night, but would take an early shower — no chance of running into Jon that time! The next day would be a busy one anyway, visiting Thomas Jefferson's home at Monticello, and the University of Virginia which he founded.

She discovered Alan still making up her bed, and went to the observation car to wait. Miguel was there as usual, and offered her a drink or coffee but she declined.

When she returned to her cabin, she felt an urgency to get her shower over with lest Jon finish his dinner and come looking for her again. So she pulled off her wig and tucked it in the lavatory pouch, removed the necklace and clothes and left them on the bed while she dashed to the shower room.

As she came back down the corridor she saw Mrs. Draper and prepared to say 'good evening' to her. But Mrs. Draper, she realized, was not coming out of her own compartment. She was coming out of Haley's. And in her hand was Roberta's necklace.

16

Actually the necklace was partly in Mrs. Draper's hand, and partly in the pocket of her dark green sweater where she had apparently stuffed it quickly on seeing Haley in the corridor. She might not have realized it was Haley, of course, without the wig, but she obviously wouldn't want anyone to see it. The clasp had come undone and one long end of the chain, as well as the pendant, protruded from the sweater pocket. Haley recognized the distinctive design immediately.

Before Mrs. Draper could get inside her own cabin and lock the door, Haley caught up to her and grabbed her arm. 'That's my necklace.'

Mrs. Draper looked startled, then puzzled, then, apparently recognizing Haley, alarmed.

'Oh, no,' she said and tried to escape

by pushing her way into the room.

Haley hung on and followed her inside cabin 'F.' 'It is too.' For a split second, she thought she sounded like a child, like the times she and her sister had quarreled over a toy.

She cleared her throat and repeated her claim. 'It's mine, or rather it belongs to a friend of mine who lent it to me. Give it back right now.'

'No, this isn't the one,' Mrs. Draper insisted, and she managed to keep her hand inside the sweater pocket, holding the necklace in place.

Haley wasn't about to give in. She yanked on the woman's arm to bring it out, and they struggled in the narrow cabin. Haley, younger and stronger, forced Mrs. Draper's hand up. The necklace dangled from her fingers, and Haley used her other hand to grab for it. 'See, it's mine.'

She let go of the woman then, but Mrs. Draper had ended up closer to the door, and Haley farther inside the room. In an instant, Mrs. Draper bent over, reached into her purse on the couch and pulled out a pistol. She pointed it directly at Haley.

If the train had not been standing still, Haley would have thought it had come off the tracks and was flying through space. Her head reeled, her breathing seemed to stop, her heart pounded. This couldn't be happening. People did not pull guns on her. She'd never even seen one this close before. Then reality set in. This was no dream. Mrs. Draper stared at her, brow furrowed, mouth compressed into a thin, determined line.

'Put the necklace on the couch,' the woman said.

Dazed, her brain fuzzy, Haley did as she was told. Even though Roberta's necklace was very expensive and she felt responsible for it, she supposed Roberta wouldn't want her to be killed over a piece of jewelry. But this didn't make any sense. She'd spoken to Mrs. Draper several times. She wouldn't really shoot her, would she?

Haley found her voice at last. 'What are you doing? What's going on?' She felt as if she had stumbled into a nightmare as unreal as any horror movie.

'Back up,' Mrs. Draper said, and Haley stepped back a few inches. 'Open the bathroom door. Go inside.'

Slowly, her mind began to work. She was to be locked in the lavatory? The situation was too bizarre. 'Why?'

'Just do as I say and I won't use this.'

Haley had a flash of memory. 'You stole my silver pin too, didn't you?'

The woman didn't reply, just waved the pistol in the direction of the lavatory door.

This just wasn't possible — it was some sort of gag. Mrs. Draper would reveal the gun was actually a cigarette lighter, return her necklace and they would laugh about it. No, that didn't seem likely. Or, how about this? She was on one of those mystery trains she'd heard of where actors pretended there had been a murder on board and the passengers were encouraged to try to find out 'whodunit.' But nothing in the brochure, or in any of the talks or the printed daily itineraries had even hinted at such a game. She had to accept the fact that her necklace and pin had really been stolen, and assume that was a real gun. She opened the door, backed into the lavatory, and almost immediately, Mrs. Draper slammed the door shut.

Haley stood still in the dark little room, body trembling. Involuntary tears clouded her eyes. What would happen to her? Her pounding heart increased its tempo until she thought she'd faint. She sat on the closed lid of the toilet and bent her head forward, trying to keep breathing.

Finally she lifted her head, swallowed and wiped her eyes with the back of her hand. Crying wouldn't accomplish anything. She'd never been a helpless female and she wouldn't be then. Anger began to replace fear. How dare that woman steal her jewelry and then threaten to kill her? She wouldn't get away with it.

After a moment, Haley felt steadier and tried to think what to do. She wondered if she could overpower Mrs. Draper, somehow get the gun away from her. She had never overpowered anyone in her life, never had to. As for taking a weapon away from someone, that was too crazy even to think about.

She took more deep breaths, made her mind work logically. All right, she was locked in a lavatory. Well, not really locked in. She felt certain the door couldn't be locked from outside, so perhaps she should just rush out and — there was that overpower thought again. And Mrs. Draper's pistol.

Then she heard voices, as if Mrs. Draper was talking to someone. Could it be the porter asking if he could turn down her bed? What if she screamed? She cracked the door open a sliver and saw Mrs. Draper sitting on the couch, the gun pointed at the bathroom door, and she was talking to someone on a cell phone. Haley heard her side of the conversation.

'I mean it. Get over here right away.' Pause. 'I don't care what you think. This is your problem and I told you before that I didn't want to be involved.' She snapped the phone closed and then slammed the lavatory door shut.

Haley backed up quickly to keep the door from smashing her nose and sat on the toilet lid again. The room had no window and it was almost pitch dark, since the light switch was not inside the cubicle, but, no doubt, outside on the wall, as in her own cabin. The only light came from that in the rest of the cabin through a narrow metal grate near the bottom of the door. But, even if she couldn't see very well, the space was too small for her to trip or fall. She could sit or she could stand up, the backs of her legs against the toilet, her face two feet away from the opposite wall, and that was about it.

She felt along the wall. Maybe there was a bell she could push to summon help. But she only touched a toilet paper roll, an expandable pouch and towels on a towel bar, just as in her own lavatory. In fact, since her room was right next door, and since — according to the diagram in the brochure — adjoining cabins were mirror images of each other, she knew she needn't try banging on the wall for help. That was her own lavatory on the other side and no one there to hear her.

She wracked her brain for other solutions, then heard the corridor door open and close and Mrs. Draper began to talk to someone who had entered. Haley pressed her ear to the door, although, since the train wasn't moving, there was little other sound to disguise their conversation.

Mrs. Draper explained to the other person that Haley had caught her with the necklace and she didn't know what to do so she had forced her into her lavatory.

The next voice belonged to a man, but it was not a deep voice, rather a bit whiny, like a petulant teenager.

'I *told* you not to steal things this time, didn't I? Now you've got the whole scheme in trouble.'

'Don't you talk to me like that, George Draper. I'm still your mother.'

'But — '

'It wasn't my idea,' the woman added. 'I never wanted any part of this and you know it.'

'Then why'd you take the gun?'

'I wish I never had. But she saw me with the necklace and grabbed it back and I knew she'd report me. I couldn't think what else to do.' She paused, but the man didn't answer that. 'If I hadn't stopped her, your whole scheme would be off anyway, wouldn't it?'

'Not if you kept your sticky fingers out of it.' His next words had a sorrowful tone. 'Geez, Mom, you been caught before lifting things. How did you expect to get away with it on this train?'

'I did last time.'

Haley remembered her conversation

with Jon when she reported the disappearance of her silver pin. Mrs. Draper — not an employee of the train company — was the thief Jon had been asked to ferret out.

Haley had missed some of the conversation, but picked up the man saying, 'Couldn't you keep your hands off stuff until we get through with this?'

'You told me you'd be through with it by Monday.'

'Not our fault the train didn't stop in Florida like we expected,' he said. 'The guys was sittin' in the van for hours waitin' and it never stopped. Now they're chasin' it and we can't do nothing until tomorrow.'

'Well, it's not *my* fault the rain storm made the train late and you've got to change your plan.'

After a long pause, George spoke again. 'Well, now you've gone and done it, we got to keep her locked up until it's over.'

'How?'

'You're the one got us into this

pickle. You're the one has to watch her.'

'But that's almost twenty-four hours from now. How will I eat, sleep, when I have to watch her? She's — '

'I'll fix it for you.'

By 'fix' did he mean he'd kill her? For a horrible moment Haley thought she was a dead woman.

Before she could react, the door was pulled open and Haley blinked into the light. But nothing happened. No shot, no sudden pain. Her eyes adjusted, and she realized the man who stood in front of her didn't hold a gun. She almost fainted with relief.

But his voice didn't match his body. He was a tall, heavily muscled man, and perhaps he didn't need to shoot her. He could strangle her with those beefy arms and giant hands. He wore jeans and a sweatshirt, not the uniform of a train employee, although he might be one. She didn't recognize him but since there were supposedly forty members in the crew, many of them working behind the scenes, that didn't surprise her. And yet, in a way, she thought she had seen him before. He looked young, twenties maybe, with small eyes in a round face. Those eyes had looked at her once before. But when, where?

'Turn around,' he barked at her, and she did as he said. 'Put your arms back here.'

She obeyed, relieved to know — for the moment at least — that he wasn't going to kill her. Instead, he was going to tie her up. Her anger returned. How dare he treat her that way? But there was nothing she could do about it. The space was too tight for any maneuvering room and his size gave him all the advantage, to say nothing of his mother behind him, presumably still holding the gun.

And Haley wore nothing but a terry cloth robe! She couldn't even think of anything to say. What did people say at times like that? Dialogue from old movies flashed through her mind, like, 'You'll never get away with this,' or, 'You'll have to kill me first.' No, not that line!

While she stayed silent, something soft went around her wrists and she imagined it was the tie to another terry cloth robe, not a rope or something stronger. He apparently had nothing else, hadn't expected to have to tie anyone up, she supposed. Those people were amateurs.

Amateurs or not, they had the better of her. Furthermore, amateurs with guns were probably a lot more dangerous — at least unpredictable — than professionals. He whipped a large scarf over her head, adjusted it across her mouth and tied it tightly behind her head. 'There,' he said, and he slammed the door shut on her once more.

The next sound she heard was a noise like something falling and then banging against the door. She imagined suitcases wedged in front of it so it couldn't open. Fortunately, the one against the door only covered up half the grate that was providing her with light and air.

'Okay,' George said again. 'Now you

see she stays there. Don't ever leave this room, 'cause you can't lock the door from outside.'

'What about meals?'

'I'll bring you something in the morning. Don't let the porter in. Say you don't want to be disturbed.' He paused, and his voice sounded farther away. 'Don't tell 'em you're sick or they'll send a doctor.'

'I don't know — '

'It'll work. Just hang on and tomorrow it'll all be over.'

'But what will we do with her then? She knows what we look like, who we are.'

'We'll have to take her with us when we go. Worry about that later.'

The door opened and closed again. Haley slumped back down on the toilet seat, frustrated and frightened. George Draper had said they'd take her with them, and then what? She shivered. She wished she hadn't quarreled with Jon. If she hadn't said she never wanted to see him again, he might have come looking for her. But not anymore. She suddenly wished she had never signed up for the trip at all. Sure, her old life had been dull, but she was pretty sure dull was better than dead.

17

Jon left the Jacksons after dinner and went looking for Haley. He had to find out why she had suddenly rejected him, why she seemed so upset and angry. He needed to get her alone and talk to her, do something to clear up that obvious misunderstanding.

He tried both club cars and then the observation car, but she wasn't in any of them. Then he went to her cabin and knocked on the door. No answer. He didn't think she was asleep yet, so he tried again and then called to her. Still no answer.

Desperate, he tried her door knob and found it turned under his hand. He pushed it open cautiously, peered around the edge, but saw no sign of her. The red dress she'd worn that night lay across the couch, which had not yet been turned into a bed. Thinking she might be in the lavatory, he stepped into the compartment a few inches and called, but still nothing. He'd already trespassed far too much, and he backed out of the room.

Perhaps she was taking an early shower. He retraced his steps to the end of the corridor and stopped in front of the shower door. He tapped on it, got no answer, and trying the knob, found it locked. He remained in the corridor and waited to see if she'd come out, but after ten minutes, his pager went off and he returned to the train office.

When he appeared at the office window, Frank looked up from the desk. 'You know that Percival Vandeveer guy you wanted to get information about?'

'Yes, I sent a FAX. Has an answer come in?'

'Yeah. New Orleans police picked up an old man answering his description. He's in a hospital now under observation.'

'Is he okay? Can he answer questions?'

'I don't know. That's all we've got so far. I'll keep on it and find out what happened.'

'What about the other one, the one here on the train that's been using Vandeveer's name and cabin? Anything on the snapshot I FAXed about *him*?'

'No, nothing on that yet. I'll let you know.' He handed over the document.

Jon retrieved the snapshot, the picture he'd taken the day before when the man was unaware, studied it for a moment and put it in his breast pocket.

'What makes you suspicious of this guy anyway?' Frank asked. 'Even if he isn't Vandeveer, there may be a good reason why he's taking the old guy's place.'

'That's what I need to learn.'

'Since you told us to keep an eye on him, I found out he always comes into the dining car after closing time and gets some food to carry back to his cabin.' Frank shrugged. 'But I guess there's no law against that.'

'No, but he leaves the train, yet doesn't get on the buses for the side trips. What's that all about?'

'Pretty strange, all right.'

'Well, thanks for the help,' Jon said. 'Keep me informed.'

He strode through the car, then through the two dining cars, where waiters were removing tablecloths and saying good night to the final passengers as they left. He walked into the next club car, then all the way back to observation. No sign of the make-believe Vandeveer. Nor of Haley, for that matter.

Next, Jon tried the sleeping car the man had been assigned to and stood for a moment at his cabin door, preparing his questions before knocking. Until he knew something concrete, or the man did something illegal, he had to use caution. But he needn't have worried: his questions went unasked. No one answered.

He summoned the porter and — after the young man rapped loudly — followed him into the cabin. There was nothing suspicious inside. Percy Vandeveer's impersonator had few clothes and only cheap toiletries. They backed out.

As for Haley, what had happened to her? Would she be on the trip to Monticello the next day? Surely she'd want to go if for no other reason than to report what she'd learned to her students. But where was she that night? He remembered she'd had dinner with Mrs. Wolski. Hoping it wasn't too late, he knocked on her cabin door.

Mrs. Wolski opened it. 'Yes?'

'Excuse me. I'm sorry to bother you so late, but I'm looking for Haley Parsons. Have you seen her since dinner tonight? Is she with you?'

'No, she tell me she will go to bed early.'

He stood still for a minute, then said, 'Well, thank you anyway,' and left.

So that was a dead end. Of course there were other people on the train whom Haley might have become acquainted with and whose cabin she might be visiting right then, but he could hardly disturb every passenger on the entire train to look for her. He sighed and headed back to the crew's quarters and his own room. He had stacks of paper waiting for him, and brochures to read about the trip to Charlottesville in the morning. Really, his first priority was the train and the job he'd been hired to do, not Haley Parsons.

Even if she returned to her own cabin eventually, she probably wouldn't speak to him, and he didn't want to make a fool of himself talking through her closed door again. He'd spend the rest of the evening finishing his work and get up early to catch Haley at breakfast. She might try to avoid him but, if he was lucky, he'd see which of the buses she boarded and get on the same one. He sat on his couch, pulled the paperwork onto his lap, and settled down to work.

★　★　★

Haley stood in the lavatory and tried to figure out what to do. Her initial fear and anxiety had given way to angry determination. She wouldn't let them get away with treating her like that. But how?

The belt of the robe tying her wrists together was soft enough not to cut into her flesh, but still tight enough that she could barely move her arms. She could lift them up and back only slightly and she could lower them to about thigh level, but not lower, so there was no way she could get them in front of her, a maneuver she'd seen in some film years before.

The scarf across her mouth moved when she flexed her cheeks and chin, but that just pushed it into her mouth where it tasted like cotton balls. She might even be able to scream with it in place if she had to but didn't want to goad Mrs. Draper into using the pistol. At least she could breathe.

Her eyes had adjusted again to the minimal amount of light, but she saw nothing that would help her escape from her prison. She thought of trying to pull down a towel bar to use as a weapon, but, since she couldn't raise her arms that high, she couldn't reach it. Turning around, she backed up to the wall with the expandable pouch and used her fingers to investigate inside, but felt nothing but sheets of paper, probably the same daily itineraries she'd stuffed into hers. The toilet paper holder was recessed and it would take stronger fingernails than hers — at least a screwdriver — to pry it loose to — to do what? In spite of the seriousness of her predicament, she had to smile at the thought of hitting Mrs. Draper over the head with a toilet paper receptacle.

She sat on the toilet lid again, grateful that — although she seemed to have no resources at her disposal — she had overcome her initial panic and could even laugh at something. She tried to get comfortable, leaning back, but the pipes behind the toilet dug cruelly into her spine. She turned sideways, leaned back against the wall with the towels, and braced her knees against the opposite wall, only inches away. Hardly comfortable, but better than the alternative.

She wondered if she might have to spend the night in that position. In fact, she was tired and had been looking forward to getting some sleep. She hadn't slept well the night before, alternately crying and fuming about Jon's two-timing her. She had made up scenarios in which she paid him back for his treatment of her, but they only pushed slumber further away, and she had tossed and turned until the sheets were a rumpled mess. But a failed romance wasn't the only cause of lost sleep. Being in mortal danger — like right then — was having the same effect. She didn't want to think about what the immediate future held. She wanted to sink into unconsciousness and not wake up until the nightmare was all over. But how could she?

What was going on? Did George and his buddies plan to rob the train? In old Westerns the bad guys wore bandannas, robbed trains, and rode off on their horses. These robbers, if that's what they were, apparently traveled in a van.

She pondered what she'd heard. Apparently the plan, whatever it was, had been originally scheduled for some place in Florida on the first night out of New Orleans. But the storm had kept the train from departing on time, and then — according to Jon — they had another three-hour delay. As a result, when the train finally started to move again, it had to make up lost time, so it didn't stop at the place George's buddies in the van expected.

So, whatever it was had been postponed to the next day, Thursday, in Richmond. But what? Were they going to put dynamite on board and blow it up like terrorists? They didn't *look* like terrorists, not the Drapers anyway. Besides if they wanted to blow up the train, they'd just leave her on board to die, not talk about taking her with them.

She closed her eyes and tried to think of some way to get free. But the vision

that rose to her mind was of dancing
with Jon after dinner the night before.
How she longed to be in his arms
again. What a fool she'd been to push
him away. At the moment, she was
willing to forgive him anything if he
would just come and rescue her. Tears
welled up again and she couldn't wipe
them away. They just dripped into the
scarf and made it taste salty.

★　★　★

The sound of someone pounding on
the door woke her. By some miracle,
she had dozed after all and — thanks to
brighter light coming through the metal
grate at the bottom of the lavatory door
— she deduced morning had arrived.
The pounding stopped, and Mrs. Draper
apparently opened the cabin door and
let someone inside.

Haley recognized the voice of the son
George. He had brought food for them
both. Well, he wasn't all bad, was he?

After a long time, with the sound of

the cabin door opening and closing a few times, George left and Mrs. Draper apparently relocked the cabin door and shoved the suitcases out of the way enough to get Haley's prison open.

'Here,' she said. 'We've got food for you.'

Haley straightened up and Mrs. Draper, obviously realizing she was helpless to do anything about the food, removed the scarf from Haley's mouth.

'Let me come out,' Haley said.

'No, you stay right there.'

'At least untie my hands.'

Mrs. Draper shook her head. 'I can't do that. Here, I'll feed you.' Still holding the gun in her right hand, she stuffed part of a blueberry muffin into Haley's mouth.

Half of it fell out again and Haley managed to say, 'Too dry.'

'Oh, you need something to drink?'

Haley nodded and Mrs. Draper reached around the doorway, where she presumably set down the muffin on the cabin's wash basin and brought up a glass half full of orange juice. She tilted it to Haley's lips and Haley drank greedily, grateful to freshen her mouth.

'Please,' Haley said. 'Untie my hands so I can eat. You can tie me up again later.'

'No, it's this way or not at all. And don't you try screaming. If you do, the gag goes back and you don't get anything to eat.' She put the glass back on the wash basin. 'No one will hear you anyway.'

Alternately getting chunks of two blueberry muffins and sips of orange juice, Haley devoured the breakfast and then tried to engage the woman in conversation.

'Does your son work for the train company?'

'No.'

'I thought if he did, you might get a discount, and that's why you took this trip before.'

'I don't need a discount. I can afford — ' She broke off, as if realizing she shouldn't tell Haley anything personal.

'If you can afford a ticket, then why

do you steal people's jewelry?' Haley asked.

'None of your business. That's enough talking now.' She reached for the scarf that had bound Haley's mouth.

'Please don't put that in my mouth again. I promise I won't scream or anything.'

The woman considered that for a moment, and then apparently decided Haley could be trusted. 'Like I said, it wouldn't do any good. The passengers have all left already, got on the buses to go to Monticello. Probably won't be anybody left on board but us.'

Monticello. How Haley had wanted to see Thomas Jefferson's home. Now she couldn't. And they were to visit the University of Virginia which he founded and where Edgar Allen Poe had lived when he was a student. But her disappointment at missing that excursion vanished in the face of what might happen to her instead.

George had said the night before that

they had to take her with them when they left the train, because she could identify them. But he hadn't said what they'd do with her afterward. Kill her?

But they didn't seem heartless. After all, they had given her some breakfast. And what did 'afterward' mean? What was going to happen that day that they were waiting for? Was there someone important on board whom they planned to kidnap? A movie star, a socialite, a millionaire, whom they could hold for ransom? Or a foreign diplomat they wanted to exchange for someone jailed in his country? No, that still made them terrorists and she couldn't believe that scenario.

'Time's up,' Mrs. Draper said, 'I won't put the gag on, but I'm locking you in again.' With that she closed the lavatory door, and Haley heard the suitcases being shoved in front of it again.

Once more she sat on the hard toilet lid, slumped her head onto her chest and sighed. She would never figure it out, probably, so why bother? The important thing was to save her own life, to get away from these people before they took her somewhere and did God knows what.

But how could she escape when she was tied up, locked in a lavatory and wearing nothing but a terry cloth robe? She fervently wished she had never decided to shower at night — daytime might have been safer. Or that she had locked up the necklace the moment she took it off instead of leaving it on the bed with her clothes. Or that she hadn't seen Mrs. Draper with the necklace. After all, Roberta was going to give it to her anyway, after the trip, so it was really her loss, not Roberta's.

Thoughts like that solved nothing. How could she get away? Who could help her? Not Jon of course, although he might wonder why she didn't go on the Monticello side trip. But, even so, he would be too busy playing tour guide to do anything about it.

Other train employees? Someone would be stationed at the exit from the train, and be replaced every few hours, but that was more than two cars away. Who else might help? The porters would make up the beds, but then they'd probably go back to their own cabins at the front of the train and read or nap until time to do whatever else they did. But George had cautioned his mother not to let the porter make up her bed the night before so Alan was unlikely to show up to unmake it. She felt guilty for having imagined Alan had stolen her pin. She'd give a year of her life to see him right then.

If not a porter, how about some other employee? Waiters might be cleaning the dining room and setting the tables, the cooks might be cooking, the laundry people washing loads of sheets, towels and table linens, all of it several cars away at the very least. She was on her own. She'd have to figure out a way to get free all by herself.

She reached her arms backward until they touched the pipes behind the toilet. She shoved them down, trying by feel to locate something sharp that might cut through the terry cloth belt that bound her. But the belt fabric was at least two inches wide and doubled. Even if she found a sharp edge and could manage to rub the belt against it, she'd be older than Mrs. Draper before she cut through all that cloth.

And then there was the blocked door. If, by some miracle, she could push the door open with those suitcases in the way, there was still the woman and her weapon. It would take another miracle to have her fast asleep on the couch, not able to see or hear her.

She needed something other than physical prowess to get her out of this mess. She would have to use her brain. Was it up to the challenge? If not, she might never see Roberta again. Or Jon. If she ever got out of this alive, she would tell him about the wig and beg him to forgive her for deceiving him.

18

Mrs. Draper's son showed up around what Haley thought must be well after noon to bring lunch, and once more she decided that her captors were little more than amateurs. In fact, Mrs. Draper asked George to untie Haley's hands and let her eat her sandwich by herself.

'You can tie her up again before you leave.'

'I can't stay,' George protested. 'I got things to do.'

'Like what?' she asked. 'You told me you had it all planned.'

'I got to learn the lay of the land and make sure the guys know what they're s'posed to do. Why can't you stay here and guard her like you been doing?'

'I need a cigarette.'

'I thought you quit.'

'I'm trying, but this business of yours makes me nervous. Besides I hate being cooped up here all the time. Just five minutes. You watch her while she eats lunch and I'll go to the vestibule and have a cigarette. Please.'

Haley heard the door open and close and then the suitcases were shoved aside and George told her to come out.

'Can I sit on the couch?' she asked. 'That toilet lid is so hard.'

He laughed, then seemed to realize she didn't have the gag in her mouth. 'Hey, where's the scarf? Where'd that go?'

'I promised your mother I wouldn't scream if she took it off. I can't breathe with it on.' She figured telling a lie to a thief was not a sin.

'Okay. Turn around.' He untied her hands and pushed her onto the couch as far from the door as possible. Then he pulled down the shade over the window. 'Here.' He handed her a paper bag that contained a sandwich wrapped in a square of aluminum foil and a thermos of coffee.

She relished the coffee and the food — salami and Swiss on rye — almost as much as the softness of the couch under her sore bottom. Between bites she tried to engage him in conversation, but he was even more taciturn than his mother had been, answering none of her questions.

She sighed. It was going to be very difficult to gain her freedom by brain-work when she had no idea what kind of business he and his buddies had in mind. All she knew was that Mrs. Draper had indicated the event — whatever it was — would take place almost twenty-four hours from the time they had kidnapped her, and that time had to be approaching fairly soon.

Was it to be while the other passengers were off the train, like robbing the mail? But no one robbed the mail any-more — except out of suburban mailboxes — it went by air, not trains. And even if it did go on a train, it wouldn't be that one which was going to spend a week just getting from New Orleans to Washington. Not that delivery that slow would surprise her.

She shook her head to dispel the notion and took another bite of her sandwich, thinking again that the mother-son couple was a far cry from real — or even movie — villains. That gave her another idea. Surely real bad guys didn't feed their prisoners. Unless, of course, they were holding her for ransom. But that made even less sense — no one in her family had a substantial amount of money to pay for her return.

Anyway, if they wanted to kidnap her, they'd have taken her off the train hours ago. The scheme George talked about was something entirely different and she had just stumbled into their web because of her necklace, nothing more. But that didn't make her current predicament any less dangerous. A sudden fear returned, making the food lodge in her throat. She took a swallow of coffee and tried to quell her queasy stomach.

The brief lunch time over, Mrs. Draper returned from her smoking break, and George ordered Haley to her feet.

She took a moment to tie her own belt tightly around her robe, not appreciating the looks George gave her whenever it gaped open to reveal her bare legs. Then he tied her hands behind her back again and left.

Mrs. Draper told her to get in the lavatory, closed the door on her and shoved at least one suitcase in front of it. Then she apparently lay down on the couch and soon Haley heard snoring. But being asleep didn't make her less dangerous so long as she still had the gun nearby, Haley's hands were tied and the door blocked.

She wished she could sleep some more herself, but she knew she had to stay awake and figure out what was going on and how to come out of it alive. But most of all, her rear hurt from the hard seat and her neck hurt from the odd angle it had held during the night.

Maybe she could get one of the

towels down and put it over the toilet lid to cushion it. She stood up, turned away from the wall and reached behind her, grasping the edge of one of the towels. She lifted her arms up and back, at the same time moving as far away from the wall as possible, pulling. Both towels came off the bar and landed on the floor at her feet. She stooped down, tried to gather them into a bundle and maneuver the bundle onto the toilet lid. Easier said than done.

Half an hour later, her arms aching from the effort, she managed to get part of one towel onto the lid, then quickly plunked herself down on it. Ah.

Pleased with her ingenuity, she relaxed and closed her eyes. But she couldn't sleep even if she wanted to. The time for the caper was drawing near. She had to figure out how to get away. Yet her mind wandered and she found herself thinking of Roberta and of the school where they both taught and of her students. Then she thought of her mother, still living alone but with many friends to keep her days full. And finally her sister who had managed to marry a pretty nice guy and have a son who was now nineteen years old. If Haley had married the first man who asked her, like Heather had, she wouldn't be in this predicament.

Then she thought of Jon. He had been way too friendly with her real self, the woman without the wig or make-up and wearing a bulky bathrobe. Why? Then, like a burst of light, a different explanation snapped on. The thought hadn't occurred to her before, but suddenly it seemed quite plausible. What if Jon really knew it was she and was just pretending he didn't? Maybe she had closed her mind to the possibility of his recognizing her because she wanted to. Suddenly the episodes in the corridor seemed very funny, even juvenile. And he was only being charming to let her try to fool him.

What if she had let him make love to her that night? Would he have backed away if she took the wig off and said,

'What you see is what you get'? Not if he was normal, he wouldn't. They'd have made love and she'd have had dinner with him instead of Mrs. Wolski the next night and they'd have made love again. The very thought of it made her dizzy with desire. Instead, she would probably die without ever having had those moments of passion with him.

She had to stop thinking of that, stop reminding herself it was her own fault she had put herself in a position where Mrs. Draper could kidnap her. Anger swelled in her chest again. She was not going to die if she could help it. She would get free somehow. They wouldn't get away with this.

She needed to plan her escape, what she'd do when they tried to take her off the train with them, either before or after whatever was going to happen.

Off the train. And she wearing only a robe. Then her brain swung into action with another idea.

She got up and went to the door. 'Mrs. Draper.'

'What do you want?'

'I need to talk to you. It's important.'

Silence. Then finally the suitcase was shoved aside and the door opened. Once more, Mrs. Draper held the gun in front of her. 'Say what you got to say quick. We don't have much time.'

'That's what I want to talk to you about. Pretty soon the passengers will come back on board.'

'So?'

'I heard your son say you're going to take me with you when you go.'

'I guess so. He thinks that's best.'

'But I'm not dressed. You can't take me off the train wearing nothing but a robe.'

Mrs. Draper was silent for a minute. 'I don't know about that.'

'Whatever he plans to do,' Haley said, 'I imagine he'll want to get away quickly as soon as it's over. And you won't be able to do that if you've got a barefoot woman in a robe to worry about.'

'I don't know — '

'Look, I have an idea. Why don't you let me get dressed now? The passengers are still gone and my compartment is right next door. It will only take a few minutes for me to put on some clothes and then, when we get off the train, I won't be so conspicuous.'

Mrs. Draper rubbed her hand thoughtfully over her chin. 'Yes, I see what you mean. George didn't think of that, did he?' She seemed to like the idea that she could one-up him.

'We need to do it soon,' Haley said, 'before the passengers return, while there's still nobody in the corridor to see us.'

Mrs. Draper frowned. 'But how am I gonna keep you from trying to get away while you do that?'

'You'll be with me.'

'I don't know. Maybe I'd better ask George first.'

'He's probably busy now. When he brought lunch, he sounded like he didn't want to be bothered with us. You don't want to upset his plans.'

Still she hesitated.

'Look,' Haley said. 'You can keep my hands tied until we get inside my cabin. Then you untie me, I get dressed, and you can tie my hands again.'

That seemed to convince her it was safe. 'Okay.'

Haley stepped out of the lavatory and followed Mrs. Draper to the door, which the woman opened cautiously before peering out. 'All right,' she said, 'you go ahead and remember I have this gun right at your back.'

Haley nodded, and they stepped out into the corridor. Her cabin door was barely four feet away and she opened it to find that the porter had hung up her red dress and remade the bed into a couch. While Mrs. Draper locked the door behind them and stood guard in front of it, Haley opened one of the plastic drawers and pulled out some underwear. Heedless of the older woman watching her, she yanked off the robe and put on the bra and panties. Next she pulled a long-sleeved maroon sweater from the second drawer and then reached into the narrow closet to unfasten her gray pants from the tiered hanger and put them on. Finally she pulled her low-heeled shoes from their usual resting place, sat on the couch and slipped into them. For a brief moment she wondered if she could hit Mrs. Draper over the head with a shoe, but the sight of the gun made her think better of it.

'You ready now?' Mrs. Draper said. 'Let's go.'

'I have to put on some makeup.' She delved into her handbag and pulled out her cosmetics bag, hurriedly applied foundation, eyeliner and lipstick, just as she had every day of this trip. She was getting pretty good at it but she wished she had a can of hair spray that she could shoot into Mrs. Draper's face and then disarm her. However, like the shoe-over-the-head idea, she dismissed it. Besides, she had a less dangerous plan in mind.

'Okay, now.'

'Oh, one more thing,' Haley said. 'My wig. I wore a blonde wig on this trip. If you want people to recognize me and not ask any questions, I'll have to put it back on.'

While Mrs. Draper thought about it, Haley held her breath.

'Okay, put on the wig.'

'It's in the lavatory.' Without waiting for permission, and praying that Mrs. Draper wouldn't follow her, she went in, reached under the blonde wig and grabbed her cell phone that was still in the pouch on the lavatory wall. She lifted up the edge of her sweater, opened the cover of the cell phone and pushed it over the waistband of her slacks, then pulled the sweater back down and grabbed the wig. What luck that she had a wig. Otherwise, she might never have managed to get the phone.

Back in the main room of her cabin, she faced the mirror over the sink and adjusted the wig carefully. Still without facing Mrs. Draper, she said, 'I should take my raincoat.' That would help conceal the bulge in the front of her slacks.

'No coat,' Mrs. Draper said.

'My purse.' Haley reached for the bag again. 'People will wonder if a woman isn't carrying a handbag.'

'Just a minute.' Mrs. Draper came close to her.

Haley held her breath. Did she see the bulge under her sweater? Mrs. Draper snatched the purse out of her hands and pulled out the cosmetics bag, billfold, address book, pen, wrist watch and sunglasses and laid them all out on the couch before she turned the bag upside down and shook it. She glanced briefly over everything, picked up the wrist watch and shoved the rest in Haley's direction.

'Okay,' she said.

Haley, breathing ragged and her heart thumping away in her chest like a jackhammer, scooped up everything and shoved it back in the bag, mentally cursing the woman for stealing yet another of her possessions.

'Turn around,' Mrs. Draper ordered and, after she did so, Mrs. Draper hung the bag over Haley's shoulder by its strap and then tied her hands behind her back again. Then she marched her out of that cabin and into her own. In minutes Haley was back in the lavatory, sitting on that damn toilet lid. The towel she had so laboriously placed over it had fallen off, but she felt like a human being again in real clothes. And maybe, with luck, she'd get a chance to call for help.

★   ★   ★

Jon stood at the door of the bus and, when it pulled into the station, was the first person to get off. His chest felt tied up in knots worrying about Haley. She had not been on either of the buses and had entirely missed the side trip to Monticello. That was not like her. She was devoted to history and had planned

267

to take lots of pictures and notes about everything she saw to share with her students back home. Why on earth had she stayed behind that day?

Maybe she was sick. That thought worried him even more, and he dashed up the steps of Seattle car and practically ran down the corridors of the next two cars. He knocked on Haley's door, and when she didn't answer, he opened it. No Haley. Trespassing be damned. He strode inside and tapped on the lavatory door. Getting no response, he opened it. Empty. He looked around. The bed was made; no clothes lay about. Two long dresses and the terry cloth robe provided by the train hung on the wall hook. He checked her drawers and closet, finding her other clothes were still there. But no purse and no wig. She was either somewhere on the train or . . . He didn't like to think of that possibility, but nothing else made sense. She had got off and was somewhere in Richmond. But why? And how on earth would he find her?

Logic told him she had to be on the train, as her coat hung in the closet. Although the weather had turned warmer that day, a cooler evening was coming, so why would she go out without a coat? Logic also told him that she was a grown woman and used to taking care of herself. If she wanted to visit the science museum or go anywhere else in the city, she could certainly do so. It was still daylight besides. What could happen to her in broad day-light? But deep in his gut, he knew something had.

19

Besides the cell phone on which she could dial nine-one-one so the police would come and rescue her, Haley had another item that could help her escape: the nail file in her cosmetics bag in her purse. She could use it as a weapon, perhaps, or as a means of cutting through the belt that held her wrists together. The trouble was, her hands were tied behind her back again and she couldn't reach either phone or file.

Still, her ploy to get Mrs. Draper to let her go to her own room next door and get dressed, had forced the woman, instead of her son, to retie her hands. Women were usually not as strong as men and couldn't tie things as tight. In fact, Haley was sure, by the very way she could flex her wrists, that Mrs. Draper had not done as good a job.

Perhaps she could somehow wriggle her hands free.

The noises both inside and outside the parked train told her that the passengers were returning and soon they might all go into the dining cars for dinner. She wished she knew what time it was, but her wrist watch belonged to Mrs. Draper at the moment. In any case, she had to hurry.

Flexing her wrists worked up to a point, but then the knot in the belt seemed to go tighter instead of looser. She felt sure that eventually it would loosen, but how long would that take?

Once more she thought of the plumbing behind the toilet. Although she hadn't felt anything sharp back there the other time she tried to cut herself loose, perhaps something else could be used. She reached her arms back as far as she could and, with the increased mobility of her wrists, was able to feel around alongside the pipes. Her fingers touched something that might be a knob or valve. Round, it stuck up from whatever it was connected to. Perhaps, if she could manage to get her wrist around it and pull, it would loosen the knot in the belt.

And if pulling on it disconnected some plumbing and started a flood, well, that might attract attention and get her rescued.

Before she could try, she heard the compartment door open and George spoke loudly to his mother. 'It's goin' down,' he said. 'You stay put here until I come back and tell you the coast is clear.'

'When will that be?'

'Soon. I'll be in the office so if you need me you can call on that phone.' He was probably pointing to the handset on the wall. 'But don't use it unless you have to. I want the guys to be able to tell me when they're through so we don't waste no time gettin' outta here.'

'Listen, George, I've been thinking. Are you sure you want to do this?'

'Yeah, the guys are all ready. They got

their garbage bags, their masks — '

'How can the seven of you rob a whole big train? I tell you, it's not going to work.'

They were going to rob the train. Haley's heart began to pound so hard she thought it could be heard. She pressed her ear to the door.

'You said your piece before, Ma. Don't give me a hard time now.'

'You won't get away with it. You'll get caught. I know you — you never did anything right in your life, always make dumb mistakes, just like your father.'

'You're a fine one to talk. What about your shoplifting?'

'I only got caught once, years ago. I learned better. I don't make mistakes anymore. But you don't have experience.'

'I'm not stupid, Ma. I planned it careful. Izzy does the back three sleeping cars and Carl does the front ones.'

'What do you mean 'does' them?'

'They go into each compartment,

273

break open the locked drawer under the couch and grab anything valuable.'

'What if there's someone in the room?'

'They won't be. They'll be in the dining cars.' He hurried on. 'Nick and Orry do the first dining car and Tim and Buzz do the other one.'

'What about the waiters?' Mrs. Draper asked.

'I told 'em they got to make the cooks and waiters come out of the kitchens and into the dining cars. One of 'em keeps an eye on them while the other is taking stuff off the passengers sitting at the tables.'

'And where will you be while all this is going on?'

'Like I said, in the train office. Every phone is connected to there. So when they're through, they call in and we jump off together and head for the van.'

'What about the girl?'

'Before I get off, I'll come back and get the girl. You can stay on board. Nobody knows you're involved.'

'I am involved. It's all my fault. I wish I'd never told you about stealing jewelry on the train. Now you got this crazy idea and it'll end up like everything else you've ever done. Only this time they'll lock you up for good.'

After a long pause, George sneered, 'Thanks for the confidence, Ma.' Then the door opened and closed again.

Haley shivered. The robbery was beginning already. She had to get her hands loose and call the police. She slid her arms backward, and managed to force her bound wrist over the valve, pulling as hard as she could. The belt got tighter and bit into her wrists. And her heavy handbag, which Mrs. Draper had slung over her shoulder before tying her hands, kept falling in her way. She stopped pulling and tried to maneuver the knot over the valve. Time after time she tried, but it kept slipping off. Her arms ached from the effort and tears of frustration welled in her eyes.

★ ★ ★

Jon raced through the cars looking for Haley's blonde head. She was nowhere. The observation car and the club cars were virtually empty while everyone was dressing for dinner. Damn. Then his pager went off and he raced back to the office.

Instead of Frank, the redhead, Abby, sat there. 'We've got more information,' she said. 'Percival Vandeveer told the police that he was robbed near the train station, bound and gagged and left behind a supply building.'

'Is he okay?'

'Apparently nothing wrong with him but a couple of bruises and a damaged ego. Because of his age, they took him to the hospital anyway just to make sure.'

John smacked his hand onto the counter. 'I was right. He was deliberately kept from getting on the train so someone else could take his place.'

'Who?' Abby asked.

'I don't know his name yet, but he's young, big. Did any information come in about the snapshot I FAXed?'

She looked through the papers on the tiny desk. 'If it did, I don't see it.'

'Never mind. Get Frank on the horn. Tell him to find the guy who took Vandeveer's place. Frank knows what he looks like. We need to check every car in the train, and I mean every one. I'll take the front half and he takes the back half. We meet here.'

Fifteen minutes later, Frank reported there was no sign of the man, and Jon realized he didn't have one missing person to worry about. He had two. He still hadn't found Haley. Perhaps she really had gone off somewhere.

After one more look in her compartment, he swung down off the train and headed for the station building. A thorough search told him she wasn't there. It was beginning to get dark by then, and he hurried on to the science museum, but that was closed for the night.

He next went to the ticket desk of the IMAX theater.

'The show is just about over,' the ticket seller told him. 'The people will be coming out any minute.'

Jon paced the floor in front of the doors, checked his watch a dozen times, and wondered what to do if she didn't come out of the theater. Where else could he look?

Suddenly the double doors of the theater opened and people poured out. He watched every person leave, then went inside and looked for her. She wasn't there.

He slammed his fist into his palm. Where the hell was she? And where was the guy who took Vandeveer's place for that matter? Wait a minute. Could he and Haley be together? No, that made no sense. She'd never been seen with him. In fact, no one had. He'd never gone into the dining cars or on any of the side trips. But there was nothing evil in that. Okay, he was a suspect in Vandeveer's mugging, but Jon didn't know that for sure and he could think of no motive for it. Why would a man rob a passenger and take his place on the train if he wasn't going to enjoy the amenities? What was his purpose?

Only one thought came to mind: something illegal. He freed his imagination to conjure up a scenario, sensible or not. The one that came sent a chill up his spine. He was the thief Jon had been asked to discover. He had stolen Haley's pin and somehow she had found out about it. He had kidnapped her to silence her. Maybe to kill her. Desperate, Jon ran across the parking lot to the street fronting the theater to hail a cab. There was nothing else to do now but head for the nearest police station.

★ ★ ★

'So, this person, this — ' The police chief — an overweight man in his fifties, a circle of tight gray curls on his otherwise bald head — looked at Jon through slitted eyes, a frown creasing his forehead, ' — this Haley Parsons, has been missing from the American Orient Express — ' He paused, stroked his chin. 'That's that private train that goes through here several times a year, isn't it?'

'Yes,' Jon answered. 'And Miss Parsons is one of our passengers and she's disappeared.'

'You her companion or something?'

'No, as I told you before, I'm the security director for the train and it's my responsibility to see that nothing happens to the passengers.' He handed over the snapshot he had taken of Haley. 'This is her picture.'

'How long she been gone?'

'Since early last evening.' Jon reasoned that it *could* be true since that was the last time he'd seen her, and besides he couldn't wait for another day. The train would be on its way to Washington soon.

'I guess that's twenty-four hours,' the sergeant agreed. 'You any idea where she might have got to?'

'No. She's from Denver and so far as

I know has never been in Richmond before and has no relatives here.'

'You searched the train?'

'Yes, two of us checked everywhere.' Actually, he'd told Frank to find Vandeveer's replacement, not Haley, but then, he'd checked pretty thoroughly himself.

'We can alert the cruisers to watch out for her if she's on the streets but — ' He shrugged.

'Have you any reports of accidents or muggings or — '

'Nope. Quiet night so far, but then it's still early. Of course this precinct is not — ' He stopped, as if by another thought. 'You could call the hospitals and inquire yourself. Let you use the phone.' He pointed to a vacant desk in the office.

'There's something else,' Jon said. 'It's possible this man — ' He removed the snapshot of Vandeveer's mugger and handed that over as well. ' — may be with her. I think he may even have abducted her.'

'Kidnapping, huh? That's a horse of a different color. Sit down, Mr. Shafer. This could take awhile.'

* * *

Jon returned to the station half an hour later in a rotten mood. Even though the police had taken his cell phone number and promised to let him know if they learned anything, he doubted they'd get results in the short amount of time left to him. And maybe he was wrong about Haley and the guy being together. Considering what illegal activity the guy might be planning, he prayed they weren't together.

* * *

Straining as hard as she could, flexing and twisting her wrists, Haley felt the knot slip over the valve at last. She began to pull again. Slowly, ever so slowly, she felt the knot loosen. Then with a jerk, it opened and her hands were free. The suddenness of the release sent her body lurching forward. Her head hit the wall with a thud.

Mrs. Draper was at the door in seconds. 'What's going on in there?'

'Nothing. I dozed off and bumped my head, that's all.'

Haley hoped the woman didn't want to go to the trouble of moving the suitcases in order to open the door to see for herself, but she scrambled back onto the toilet lid and put her hands behind her, just in case. She was no longer afraid of the woman, but she didn't want her plan scuttled then. After a few moments passed and she heard no sound of suitcases being shoved aside, Haley decided all was clear. She removed her handbag from her shoulder and placed it on the floor, then stretched her aching arms and rubbed her shoulders. At last she could move them freely, but she had no time to enjoy the feeling.

She pulled the cell phone out of her slacks and turned it on. But how could she talk to the police without Mrs. Draper's hearing? If she could hear the conversation Mrs. Draper had with her son, the woman could hear hers.

She picked up one of the towels, doubled it over twice and pushed it against the grate in the bottom of the door, then pulled the second towel over her head like a tent. She faced the far wall and pressed the three numbers.

A man's voice. 'Colorado Highway Patrol. What's your emergency?'

Haley spoke in a loud whisper. 'I've been kidnapped and locked in a bathroom on the American Orient Express.'

'You're what? Speak up. I can hardly hear you.'

Then it struck her. He had said, 'Colorado.' But of course. That's where her cell phone assumed she was. How could he help her? Yet nine-one-one was the national emergency number, wasn't it? She spoke as loudly as she dared. 'I'm on the American Orient Express train parked in a station in Richmond,

Virginia, and I've been kidnapped and they're robbing the passengers.'

She stopped again. That was so far-fetched, even she could hardly believe it.

* * *

A sergeant poked his head in the police chief's office door. 'Nine-one-one dispatcher has a problem.'

'What kinda problem now?' He sighed. 'That Ursula — she's new on the job, always got to ask questions.'

'Colorado Highway Patrol told her some woman called,' the officer continued, 'said a gang is robbing the passengers on the Orient Express. Dispatcher thinks it's a gag, but she sent a black-and-white anyway. Wants to know did she do right.'

'What?'

'Hey,' the officer said, 'didn't that security guy was here a while ago — Shafer — say something about the Orient Express?'

285

The chief leapt to his feet. 'Call him on his cell phone and tell him what's happening. But first, tell Ursula to get every cruiser over there. Now!'

20

Noises came from the main part of the cabin and Haley had to strain to hear the nine-one-one operator.

'What makes you think the train is being robbed?'

'I overheard them planning it.'

'How?'

'They kidnapped me and I'm locked in a bathroom — '

'On the train?'

'Yes, cabin 'F' in the Istanbul car.'

'Where's the train going?'

'It's not moving now. It's parked behind the old railroad station.'

Haley didn't hear the answer to that, because the door opened and Mrs. Draper grabbed her from behind.

Damn. Then it occurred to her: she could have kept Mrs. Draper out. Being closed in all those hours — plus the fact that she'd never locked her own lavatory door — had made her forget the room had a lock on the inside.

Mrs. Draper pulled the towel from Haley's head, taking the wig with it, and tried to snatch the phone out of Haley's hand. Haley stretched her arm as far as she could in the cramped space, waving it back and forth out of Mrs. Draper's reach. They struggled, Haley screamed and Mrs. Draper swore.

Haley picked up the blonde wig from the floor, kept her back to the woman and pushed. She backed them both out of the lavatory and into the main part of the cabin. Able to move more freely, Haley swung around and jammed the wig on Mrs. Draper's head, only backwards so the long fall of blonde hair covered her face. She gave the woman a violent shove and Mrs. Draper landed on the couch, where she snatched the wig from her face and scrambled to find the gun she'd dropped during the struggle.

Haley dashed toward the door at the

same time she shouted one more word — 'Help' — into the cell phone, and then the gun appeared in Mrs. Draper's hand.

'Get back in the bathroom,' she said.

But Haley stood between her and the door to the corridor and ignored the order. Mrs. Draper wouldn't shoot her. She had fed her the muffins, had removed the gag from her mouth and let her get dressed. She might be a kleptomaniac and a poor role model, but she wasn't a murderer.

Haley reached behind her back and felt for the lock, turned it, grasped the door knob. She had to turn around to open the door and in that second, Mrs. Draper reached out to grab her sweater, trying to stop her.

'Don't go out there,' Mrs. Draper said. 'It's dangerous. Wait with me until it's all over. We won't hurt you if you do that.'

Haley didn't answer. All she could think of was that she had to get away, had to get off the train. She pulled her sweater loose, slammed the door shut behind her and ran through the car, her cell phone still clutched in her hand and someone on the other end saying something she couldn't understand. She didn't want to stop, but she put the cell phone to her ear, only then she heard nothing. She yanked open the heavy door and plunged into the vestibule between cars, pulled open the door to the next sleeping car, then plunged down that corridor. One more door and she'd be at the office in the Seattle car.

Breathless, she dashed up to the window. No usual train employee there. George. Of course. He'd told his mother that's where he'd be. Haley ducked out of sight, hoping he hadn't seen her, wondering for an instant what had happened to the rightful attendant, then pushed through the door to the vestibule once more and rushed through the doorway toward the station platform.

She had taken only the first step to get off the train when an arm went around her neck and another around her waist and she was dragged backward into the car.

'What you doin' loose?' George yelled.

Out of the frying pan —

'Where's my ma? You didn't hurt her, did you?'

Great! The vicious robber was concerned about his mother. And this bumbling idiot had managed to engineer a holdup?

'She's all right,' Haley squeaked in spite of his arm across her throat. 'I just want to get off the train.'

'No one's gettin' off till I say so. Now you made me leave the office and my guys are prob'ly callin' in.' He shoved Haley toward the door to the sleeping car she'd just come through. 'You're goin' back.'

He grabbed the phone from her hand and stuffed it in his pocket, shoved her in front of him and pulled her arms back. He was large and all muscle. She was no match for him. Holding both her wrists in one large paw of a hand, he marched her back through the cars, back to Istanbul car and cabin 'F.'

* * *

Jon stepped up into the train, his brain registering the fact that no porter or other attendant stood at the entrance to check whoever boarded. Why? What was going on? He stood still for a moment, listening, but heard only the hum of conversation. Still, the hair on the back of his neck rose. Something was up.

He stepped down again and began to walk the length of the platform toward the front of the train. Dim lights from the club car windows revealed no one inside. Next came one of the dining cars. Lamps on every table, in addition to the fancy brass fixtures on the walls, illuminated the astounding scene. A man in a mask — a Bill Clinton mask — stood in the aisle and guests were removing rings, watches and wallets and dropping them into a large black plastic bag held by the masked man. Another, this one wearing a Richard Nixon mask, stood guard over a group of waiters and cooks in the corner.

Unbelievable.

He hurried forward along the platform to the next dining car. Same scene only different masks on the robbers.

He turned and hotfooted it back to the open door of Seattle car. Senses alert, he climbed the steps carefully, made no sound. He turned left into the car and peered cautiously into the office. No one. Growing bolder, he leaned his head in the little window. Crammed under the narrow desk was Abby, hands and feet tied, a gag across her mouth. He saw her frightened eyes pleading with him.

He opened the door and rushed inside, pulled the gag from the girl's mouth. She started to speak but he stopped her with a finger on her lips.

'Don't move and don't speak loudly. They're robbing the passengers in the dining cars. I'm going to untie your hands but I don't want you to get up. I'll hand you the outside phone and I want you to call nine-one-one.'

She put her freed hand out for the handset. 'Where are you going?' she whispered.

'I've got to try to stop them.'

'But — ' She didn't finish her sentence because she had already punched in nine-one-one and begun to report the problem.

And what could Jon do, anyway? He was unarmed and there were — he didn't know how many — with guns. And where was Haley? Was she part of the gang? Was she behind one of those masks, or had she left the train and was waiting in that VW van, maybe the getaway driver? The thought that Haley might have had anything to do with it clutched at his gut and almost made him sick.

He swung down off the train again. The only open vestibule door was that one. Unless they knew how to open the others, they'd have to exit there. Maybe he could ambush them when they tried to leave. Maybe he could find help in the station.

Sirens screamed in the distance, got louder. My God, that had to be the fastest nine-one-one response on record. A moment later, brakes screeched and officers, weapons drawn, ran toward the train. Jon waved his arms in the air, yelled at them to show where they could board.

Next he had to find the van. Where had they parked it? If Haley was in it . . .

His cell phone rang.

'Mr. Shafer,' the officer on the other end said, 'that lady you were looking for — she called nine-one-one, said she's locked up on the train, something like, 'Istanbul,' whatever that is.'

He didn't wait to hear more. Teeth clenched, he jumped on board, headed for the back of the train, for Istanbul car. He had to find her.

★ ★ ★

295

No way would Haley allow herself to be locked in that lavatory again. When she and George reached the door to the cabin, she kicked backwards, twisted her body downward so he had either to bend over her back or let go of her. He swore and his arm lost its hold. They struggled in the corridor, and Haley, kicking and screaming, tried to scratch his face with her too-short nails. Suddenly, she heard pounding feet and someone leaped at George from behind. Jon.

Haley backed out of the way. The two men fought, slamming one another against the windows on one side and against the wooden doors and wall on the other. Jon apparently knew a lot about martial arts, because Haley saw some moves that she recognized from Jackie Chan films. In no time, the battle was over. George lay immobile on the floor. Haley threw herself into Jon's arms.

21

Outside, sirens still screamed and people shouted. After a long moment in Jon's arms, Haley backed away and ran a hand over her short hair, ready to explain why she had suddenly become a brunette. But he seemed not to notice anything different about her. Leaving George where he lay, Jon led Haley back to the club car.

'But Mrs. Draper — '

'Who?'

'This — this person — ' Haley pointed to George on the floor of the corridor. ' — he's George Draper and his mother is the person who kidnapped me.'

Jon's facial expression underwent a change, showed he understood the connection.

'She's the one who stole my silver pin and now she's got my wrist watch and

Roberta's necklace too.'

'Where — '

Haley didn't let him finish. 'Unless she got off the train, she's right there in cabin 'F'.'

Jon backed up, then pounded on the door of the cabin.

'Be careful,' Haley said, 'she has a gun.'

One hand pushing Haley behind him, Jon backed off, moved to the side of the door.

Mrs. Draper opened it and Haley, peering around Jon's body, saw with relief the woman wasn't holding the weapon.

Jon entered the compartment, Haley clinging to his coat tail. 'I think you have some things that don't belong to you.'

Mrs. Draper, after first eyeing Haley, turned and opened the wooden drawer under the couch. She pulled out a felt bag and Haley snatched it from her. The pin, necklace and wrist watch lay inside.

'That's not all,' Jon said. 'This isn't the first time you've robbed passengers, is it?'

Mrs. Draper sank down on the couch and stared into her lap. 'Only a couple of things. I only did it once, on the trip before this one. I'll give everything back. I promise.'

'Where's the gun?' Jon asked.

She reached into the corner of the couch and brought it out, handed it to him. 'It isn't loaded. I took out the bullets. I didn't want anyone to get hurt.'

Oh, great, and Haley had spent all those hours thinking she was in mortal danger. Not at the end, of course, but she felt used anyway. Now the woman just looked pitiful.

'Get up,' Jon said, and, moments later he marched her back through the sleeping cars. Haley followed.

When they reached the Seattle car, police officers were already hauling off the handcuffed, incompetent train robbers and shoving them into squad cars.

In the dining cars, passengers were still seated at the tables, but waiters were pulling out jewelry and wallets from black plastic bags and returning the briefly-stolen items. Other police officers — including some in plain clothes — were asking questions. Jon seemed to know the right person to talk to and, in a few minutes, Mrs. Draper too was handcuffed and led off the train.

Jon turned back to Haley. 'We're to wait in the club car,' he said, and took her hand to lead her back.

They sat together on one of the short sofas and Haley immediately told Jon about her ordeal. 'I overheard George tell his mother that they were supposed to rob the passengers somewhere in Florida, but because of the storm, the train didn't stop there.'

As soon as she finished her narrative, Jon filled her in on what he knew, that apparently George Draper had taken Percival Vandeveer's place on the train. 'He not only looked and acted suspicious, but, when I recognized the same

VW van at every stop, I knew something was up. I just didn't know what.'

'How did the other six get on board?' Haley asked. 'What happened to the person who usually manned the outside door whenever the train was stopped?'

'It was a woman and George tied her up in the lavatory of the Seattle car.'

'But those doors don't lock from outside — '

'That was the one clever thing they did. They had a special padlock that fit over the outside knob and kept it from turning.' He paused. 'You can buy anything at Radio Shack.'

Haley laughed. 'You're teasing me again.'

He put his arm around her and kissed her.

Haley touched her hair. 'How did you know it was me George had hold of when you found us in the corridor? Or were you just rescuing any damsel in distress?'

'Of course I knew it was you. I went

straight for your car.'

'But I wasn't wearing the wig. It came off in my struggle with Mrs. Draper.'

'I've always known you wore a wig.'

'What?'

'Well, almost always. I figured it out that first night when I saw you come out of the shower room.'

'In that corridor with almost no light?'

'In that not-all-that-dark corridor.'

'But I look so different when I'm wearing the wig and make-up.'

'Not really. Besides, I worked for the F.B.I., remember? I know a wig when I see one.'

'But you acted as if you didn't. You flirted with me as if I were someone else.'

'I thought you were playing a game. I can go along with a gag.'

'You thought I did it deliberately?'

'Why not? I loved those little rendez-vous we had. I liked Caroline with her southern accent.'

'Not a very good one, apparently.'

'I thought it charming of you to introduce that playful element into our relationship.' He kissed her on the tip of her nose.

'Then you don't mind that I'm not really a blonde?'

'Not at all. I've never been particularly turned on by blondes.'

'But I'm almost bald!' She told him about the incident with the bubble gum and how the hairdresser had had to cut off almost all her hair. Yet, as she rubbed her head, she realized that two weeks had made a difference already. She could almost twist a curl around her finger.

'I like your natural hair,' Jon said. 'You're beautiful the way you are.'

Haley wanted to snuggle against his chest, but other passengers, and a bartender, came into the car, began talking about being robbed and questioned by the police.

'Why do you suppose they decided to rob the passengers at dinner?' Haley asked Jon.

'To control things better. With most everyone in the two dining cars, they could rob them all at once.'

'Were their guns loaded? Mrs. Draper said hers wasn't.'

'I don't know. I didn't hear any shots fired. I guess the police disarmed them while I was finding you.'

Haley thought of something else. 'Where were you when I was locked up? Didn't you try to find me?'

'Of course. I first looked into your room last night and saw your dress on the bed and thought you were in the shower.'

'You didn't wait for me to come out?'

'I did for awhile, but then I was paged and finally I decided not to bother you anymore that night. You'd been very angry with me — '

'Because I thought you were flirting with another woman — me.'

'I really kicked myself the next day for not staying by that shower door.'

'But I wasn't in the shower anymore. I'd been kidnapped by then.'

'I assumed I'd see you on the bus to Monticello. I never doubted that you'd want to go there.'

'I did want to and now I've missed it. I was locked up in the lavatory of Mrs. Draper's cabin the whole time.'

He grinned. 'Don't worry. I'll take you back some day so you can see Monticello.'

Haley didn't comment, but she liked the idea that he wanted to see her again after this was all over.

'So this afternoon when we got back from the side trip, I looked in your room again and this time your purse and wig were gone. I decided that meant you must have left the train, so I went to the museum and the theater looking for you and finally to the police.'

'I was wearing nothing but that terry robe until late afternoon when I persuaded the woman to let me get dressed.'

'That was very clever of you.'

Haley grinned at him. She liked being considered clever, even though, to her mind, she had made many mistakes.

But then, she wasn't a detective, was she? Small town schoolteachers knew nothing about escaping from kidnappers and stopping a robbery.

'I knew if I could get in my own cabin I could get my cell phone and call the police.'

'When I couldn't find you anywhere, and the guy impersonating Vandeveer was missing as well, I thought he might have abducted you — or — '

'Or what?'

'Or that the two of you were in the scheme together.'

Haley pushed away from him. 'You thought that?'

'Only for a moment,' Jon added hurriedly. 'When I talked to the police captain I told him I thought you might have been kidnapped, not that you were involved in anything illegal.'

'I'm glad to hear it.' She settled back into the seat. 'So your having told them about me helped when I called nine-one-one. They realized my call wasn't a joke.'

He took her hand in his. 'By the way,

I just want to point out that you were able to call for help because you had a modern piece of technology. For a person who prefers the past to the present, how does it happen that you even own a cell phone?'

Haley squirmed and looked down into her lap. 'Well, loving the past doesn't mean handicapping oneself in the present. I have to drive a car, don't I? And use a computer at work.' She paused. 'And I happen to like Velcro.'

As he laughed, a police officer strode up to them. 'The lieutenant wants to talk to you now.'

Jon got to his feet, holding out his hand for Haley. 'I guess it's our turn.'

'Will I see you later then?'

'I'm not sure. After I answer their questions, I'll have tons of paper work to do. But I'll see you first thing tomorrow.'

Haley followed Jon, but once in Seattle car, the officer directed her to a plainclothes detective and Jon was escorted somewhere else. She watched him leave, wishing he'd said he'd definitely be back later that night. There was still so much she wanted to say, and the train was leaving for Washington in the morning. The tour, her vacation, this adventure, would all be over in a matter of hours.

22

Haley woke with a start and saw a lighter sky outside her window. She sat up and stretched, realizing that her bed had never been made up — probably the porters had been too busy answering police questions during the time they normally made up the beds — and she had fallen asleep, still fully clothed, on the couch.

As she pulled off her slacks and sweater and went to the shower room at the end of the car, she remembered Jon leaving her the night before, telling her he had paper and other work to do and would see her in the morning. The memory of their long talk the night before cheered her, gave her hope for the future.

Roberta had been right that she'd meet someone on the train. But she might have met him anyway, because he preferred her looks without the blonde wig.

On the other hand, if it hadn't been for the wig, she wouldn't have been able to get the cell phone and call the police.

Dressed in her traveling suit, she pulled down her suitcase and packed, stuffing the wig in her tote-bag, ready for the porter to take it off the train when they reached Washington. She took her handbag with her to the dining car for breakfast, and looked around for Jon, but he wasn't there. She felt a twinge of worry start, then sat at a small table with Mrs. Wolski, who seemed to recognize her instantly even without the wig. Together they had a good laugh about how the kindergarten children had almost halted her vacation.

After breakfast Haley went to the office and waited in line while passengers settled up their bills for drinks they ordered in addition to the complimentary wine at dinner, for any purchases they might have made, like the terry cloth robes or a polo shirt with the AOE logo, and, of course the gratuity for the crew. When it was her turn, the girl in the office handed her a note. On it, Jon had scribbled, 'I'll meet you outside the station. Don't leave without me.' Her worry evaporated.

The train pulled into the station, porters opened doors and put the portable steps in place and began to help passengers to detrain. People were saying goodbye to the new friends they'd made, exchanging addresses and even hugging one another. She exchanged addresses with Mrs. Wolski, the Ellisons, even the honeymooning couple. The porters and other employees gathered outside to say goodbye and to answer questions about where to find their luggage and how to get to their destinations.

Haley walked slowly down the platform toward the waiting room, still turning her head constantly, looking for Jon but without success. When she finally walked through the entire terminal and reached the street, she retrieved her two pieces of luggage and stood on the sidewalk to wait. He'd said he'd meet her there. But after ten minutes, watching others gradually getting into taxis, she felt her doubts resurface. Perhaps, like many other men in her life before him, he didn't really mean what he said. Perhaps, for him, the romantic interlude was over. He'd met a woman, tried to make love to her, made her care for him, and now he would move on to his next conquest. Tears clouded her eyes.

Then a touch on her elbow made her turn around.

'Jon,' was all Haley could say, her anxiety receding like an ocean wave.

'Did you think I'd forgotten you?' he asked. 'Not in a million years.' He pulled her away from the side of the building. 'We don't need a taxi. I have a car.'

He took her suitcase and with his other hand under her elbow propelled her down the sidewalk. He stopped in front of the curb and opened the door of a long white limousine.

Haley got in. 'Boy, they really treat you right.'

'No, it's not a perk I get from the company.' As he climbed in after her and closed the door, Haley wondered what he meant by that, but didn't have a chance to ask.

'When do you have to go home?' he asked.

'My flight leaves at four o'clock from Reagan National.'

'Oh, good, we have plenty of time then.' He leaned forward and told the driver to go to the mall, then settled back again. 'You have to see the cherry trees.'

Indeed there seemed to be cherry trees everywhere. Haley all but pressed her nose to the window staring at the thousands of trees, looking like clouds on stilts, that sprouted from every street corner.

The limo stopped and Jon helped her out. 'He'll follow us,' Jon said, 'and pick us up at the tidal basin. It's better to walk.'

The sky was a brilliant blue with only a few puffy white clouds and the air was warm and smelled fresh, a perfect spring day.

Haley pulled her camera out of her

bag and began snapping pictures. The Washington Monument, the Lincoln Memorial, the reflecting pool — how she wished she could stay longer. But she'd have wonderful pictures to remember it all, and to share with her students.

They reached the tidal basin and Haley saw with delight that it was ringed with cherry trees, all heavy with huge pinkish-white blossoms, the branches arching over the sidewalk that edged the basin and even dipping down, almost touching the water. They walked under an archway of glistening petals.

The sun shone, the air smelled like flowers, and thousands of people, or so it seemed — housewives pushing strollers, students, office workers postponing the return to their jobs after lunch — ambled along the path under the trees or sat on the occasional wooden bench or the grassy bank.

'Tomorrow is the Cherry Blossom Festival,' Jon said. 'Why don't you stay for that? It's only Friday and you don't have to be back at school until Monday morning. Stay here two more days.'

'No, I'd better not. I need to prepare — '

'Whatever you need to do can wait. I want you to stay here with me, maybe pick up where we left off that night.'

Haley remembered only too well those moments in his arms, when — had she not been afraid her wig would come off — they might have made love. She didn't answer, found a vacant bench and sat down.

He joined her. 'I think we should explore the possibility of staying together.'

Haley's heart did a flip-flop. He cared for her. And she wanted to be with him, too. Could she really be in love? 'I hate to sound like a cliché, but this is so sudden. We only met a week ago.'

'In one of those old movies you're so fond of, a week was enough for Cary Grant and Eva Marie Saint in *North by Northwest*. And,' he added, 'they met on a train.'

'But — '

'And in *An Affair to Remember*

weren't Cary Grant and Deborah Kerr on the ship only a week before they decided to dump their fiances and meet again in six months?'

Haley considered herself a realist, and practical thoughts filled her mind. 'Those were only movies. In real life — '

'We can have six months too, to make sure, but not apart from each other.'

'When I live near Denver and you live in Portland, or is it Washington?'

'Remember, I just took the job with the train company to try to find who was stealing things from passengers. My father is a friend of the owner, so I took time off to help.'

'But before that you worked for the F.B.I. and some other corporation and you don't even work for the train company.'

'I have my own business. Dad's still C.E.O. but I pretty much run things now.'

'Is that the company your father owned that you didn't want to work for?'

'I used to think it was too dull, but now I enjoy the challenge.'

'But your company is in Portland.'

He took hold of her hands and looked deep into her eyes. 'Haley, I think I'm in love with you, but I don't want to rush into anything any more than I think you do. I had one bad marriage, you know, and this time I want to be very sure.'

Marriage. He had said marriage. But how could that work when they lived in different cities? Yet, if they really loved each other . . .

She swallowed hard, tried to compose her thoughts. 'I think that's a very good idea.'

'Would you consider moving to Portland? I'm sure they need good teachers there too.'

She hesitated and he added, 'Or, since we have a plant in Denver, I could make that my headquarters.'

The thought of Jon doing that for her, of having him nearby made her heart race again. She searched her brain for the right thing to say. 'Moving your headquarters would probably be terribly inconvenient, expensive — '

'I can manage it.'

'What kind of company do you own?'

'Food packaging. Crackers, mostly.'

Crackers. Then it hit her. His name was Shafer. Shafer Crackers was practically a household word. Their slogan cropped up as a puzzle on *Wheel of Fortune* and the answer on *Jeopardy*. It was a multi-billion dollar company and he must be worth . . .

He seemed to have read her mind. 'I don't really have to work, but I like what I'm doing. And I really can run the business from Denver as easily as Portland. Unless you'd like to move to the Northwest.' He grinned. 'I like kids too. I think we have lots more in common than sweet music and old movies.'

She could hardly put words together. She knew that they wouldn't need six months to realize they were meant for each other. But she decided to tease him one more time.

'You lied to me. You kept changing identities — you pretended to be a train employee — '

'Well,' he interrupted, 'you changed identities too. First you were a blonde model — '

' — and you were a train employee — '

' — then you were a schoolteacher — '

' — you were a detective — '

' — and you were Caroline — '

' — and now you're a cracker baron.'

He laughed and kissed the palms of her hands. 'Well, it was my turn.'

THE END

We do hope that you have enjoyed reading this large print book.

Did you know that all of our titles are available for purchase?

We publish a wide range of high quality large print books including:
Romances, Mysteries, Classics
General Fiction
Non Fiction and Westerns

Special interest titles available in large print are:
The Little Oxford Dictionary
Music Book, Song Book
Hymn Book, Service Book

Also available from us courtesy of Oxford University Press:
Young Readers' Dictionary
(large print edition)
Young Readers' Thesaurus
(large print edition)

For further information or a free brochure, please contact us at:
Ulverscroft Large Print Books Ltd.,
The Green, Bradgate Road, Anstey,
Leicester, LE7 7FU, England.
Tel: (00 44) **0116 236 4325**
Fax: (00 44) **0116 234 0205**

Other titles in the
Linford Romance Library:

DARK SUSPICION

Susan Udy

When Aunt Jessica asks Caitlin to help run her art gallery while she is in hospital, Caitlin agrees. She hadn't bargained on having to deal with a series of thefts, however — or Jessica's insistence that Caitlin's new employer, Nicholas Millward, must be responsible. Nicholas is as ruthless as he is handsome, but would he really stoop to theft? And what can Caitlin do when she finds herself in the grip of a passion too powerful to resist?

HER SEARCHING HEART

Phyllis Mallet

A proposal of marriage from Robert, whom she does not love, brings Valerie face to face with a frightening question — is she incapable of falling in love? She rejects Robert and flees to the tranquility of Cornwall, hoping to find the answer; but when she meets Bruce and his motherless young daughter Mandy, she discovers new and disturbing emotions deep in her heart — and finds the answer to her question . . .

HEAD OVER HEELS

Cindy Procter-King

Magee Sinclair keeps making costly blunders at her family's advertising agency, so when handsome Justin Kane, head of CycleMania, needs her to pose as his girlfriend for the weekend in exchange for a lucrative campaign, she has little choice but to say yes. Justin needs to cement a deal with Willoughby Bikes by impressing the Willoughbys while they bike trails together. But Magee has landed herself in major trouble — she doesn't know one end of a mountain bike from the other . . .

BACHELOR BID

Sarah Evans

City slicker Benedict Laverton is billed as top prize at the Coolumbarup Bachelors' Ball. To escape the ordeal, he persuades one of the organizers, Rosy Scott, into bidding for him with his own money. But Rosy gets carried away, bidding a cool $10,000 . . . When she goes on stage to claim her man, Rosy not only has to face Benedict's stunned disbelief, she has to kiss him too — a kiss which is spectacular enough to convince her that getting involved with Benedict will end in disaster . . .

SECRET SANTA

Anne Ryan

Jade is a journalist, attached to her boyfriend, Brad, but impossibly drawn to photographer Carl. With Christmas approaching, an exotic Secret Santa gift at work confuses her further, but why does Carl run a mile whenever the heat starts to sizzle between them? Family problems add to Jade's seasonal blues — can she find contentmant before the big day arrives . . . ?

SURGEON IN PORTUGAL

Anna Ramsay

'A strong dose of sunshine' is the prescription for Nurse Liz Larking, recovering from glandular fever. And a villa in the Algarve seems the ideal place to recuperate, even if it means cooking for the villa's owner, eminent cardiac surgeon Hugh Forsythe: brilliant, caring, awe-inspiring — and dangerously easy to fall in love with. Liz soon realises that this doctor is more potent than any virus — and ironically, it seems he could just as easily break a heart as cure one . . .